Praise for Hannah March's
Robert Fairfax mysteries

"[March] is adept at delineating characters with just a few telling phrases. . . . A well-paced, exciting book."
—The Charlotte Austin Review

"A gloriously rich tale of London at its grandest and seamiest, well told, at a cracking pace."
—The *Evening Chronicle* (Newcastle upon Tyne)

"A clever and accomplished first novel . . . witty and convincing; for fans of period dramas such as *Moll Flanders* and *Tom Jones*, this will slip down like a cup of sherbet."
—*Scotland on Sunday*

"Well written with a great deal of self-assurance. I liked the period detail and the characterizations of the large cast of suspects."
—Deryn Lake, *Shots*

Also by Hannah March

The Complaint of the Dove

The Devil's Highway

A MYSTERY OF GEORGIAN ENGLAND

Hannah March

A SIGNET BOOK

SIGNET
Published by New American Library, a division of
Penguin Group (USA) Inc., 375 Hudson Street,
New York, New York 10014, U.S.A.
Penguin Books Ltd, 80 Strand,
London WC2R 0RL, England
Penguin Books Australia Ltd, 250 Camberwell Road,
Camberwell, Victoria 3124, Australia
Penguin Books Canada Ltd, 10 Alcorn Avenue,
Toronto, Ontario, Canada M4V 3B2
Penguin Books (N.Z.) Ltd, Cnr Rosedale and Airborne Roads,
Albany, Auckland 1310, New Zealand

Penguin Books Ltd, Registered Offices:
80 Strand, London WC2R 0RL, England

Published by Signet, an imprint of New American Library, a division of Penguin
Group (USA) Inc. Originally published in Great Britain by Headline Book Publishing.

First Signet Printing, November 2003
10   9   8   7   6   5   4   3   2   1

PUBLISHER'S NOTE
This is a work of fiction. Names, characters, places, and incidents either are the
product of the author's imagination or are used fictitiously, and any resemblance to
actual persons, living or dead, business establishments, events, or locales is entirely
coincidental.

For Bill and Angela

One

The body of the man was suspended some twenty feet in the air. It swung with a slight pendulum motion in the east wind that came tumbling across the bare black fields, here on the lonely reaches of the Great North Road.

The clothes in which he had been hanged, and then brought here to be gibbeted, still clung to him in strips and tatters. Indeed, they had lasted better than he. As the carriage rattled past, Robert Fairfax gazed from the window and saw a crow alight on the crossbar of the gibbet; but the bird was only spying out the land. It did not bother with the corpse dangling below it. Meager pickings, now.

Hard to believe, Fairfax thought, that this blackened horror had ever been a human being—a man who had been nursed by a mother, had known the pleasure of food and drink and fire, had had his loves and fears and hopes. And yet . . . and yet in the way the body lazily twisted in its iron bands as the carriage trundled below it, Fairfax could almost fancy a kind of greeting; a ghastly good day to the passing travelers from a fellow who was going nowhere.

Sir Edward Nugent, who had been half dozing in the opposite seat of the post chaise, roused himself and looked out.

"Hm. Been there since the Lent assizes, I fancy." He grunted and settled himself again. "Supposed to set an example, though I misdoubt it does."

"A highway robber?" Fairfax watched the grim shape recede into the distance. The gibbet post was set about with iron spikes to prevent the criminal's relatives from climbing up to retrieve the body for a decent burial. Against the lemon-white October sky they gave the gibbet the look of some bristling nightmare tree.

"Likely enough in these parts. Don't be sentimental, Fairfax. There's one such rogue who's been plaguing the roads about my country since late last year, and I'd gladly see him swinging. The highway between Huntingdon and Stamford is his favorite hunting ground. A dozen robberies to my knowledge; some quiet folk are too feared to stir abroad. A good friend of mine was held up by the knave at pistol point in broad daylight. One doughty old fellow, a farmer in his cart, refused to pay up and was used very roughly. 'Twas after that the justices put a hundred-pound price on the fellow's head. One hundred pounds' reward for the apprehension, or information leading to it. Usually these villains are known to other reprobates, at least. But this fellow has the devil's own elusiveness. Plies his damnable trade alone, and disappears into the wilds leaving nary a clue."

"Has he killed?" Fairfax asked.

"Not yet. But what's to prevent him? Highway robbery's a hanging offense, and he knows he'll dangle, blood or no. That's why I want the fellow caught."

"Between Huntingdon and Stamford . . . Isn't that the road that lies ahead of us?"

Sir Edward gave a deep bay of laughter. "Of course. Best hide your pocket watch in your boot, Fairfax, and say your prayers. Nay, nay, I warrant we'll get to Cheyney Hall safe and sound. I was born with a caul, you know; I'm generally lucky."

Well, I am lucky too, Fairfax thought—lately at least. The profession of private tutoring, which he had never intended for himself, had turned out moderately well. Having to extricate his first young gentleman pupil from a charge of murder, as he had had to do last year, was not a part of the job he had bargained for, but somehow he had crowned that with success, and won golden opinions from his pupil's father. The trouble with tutoring young gentlemen—bear-leading, as it was disrespectfully called—was that they very soon reached an age when the bear-leader was no longer required, and they could be turned loose. And so it had happened this summer. Robert Fairfax, with no home, family, or fortune of his own, had shaken hands with his pupil for the last time, and turned to face the unfriendly world again.

But he did have a warm recommendation from his former employer—and a wealthy family was prepared to engage him as tutor for their two young boys on the strength of it. They were set to return to their Surrey seat from Ireland at the end of the summer. Relief turned to dismay. The return was postponed until Christmas, perhaps the new year, depending on the weather for the sea crossing. The family was in the process of marrying off an elder daughter to an Irish peer with estates all over Kerry and Cork—maybe there *were* Kerry and Cork—and such important business naturally had the first claim. Fairfax must shift for himself until then—which was easier said than done.

Into the choppy sea of his perplexity swam the figure of Sir Edward Nugent, baronet, of Cheyney Hall, Northamptonshire.

Sir Edward had no dull sons in need of polishing. He was a widower with two daughters. But he had heard of Fairfax's scholarly accomplishments, and sought him out because of them. (Which put Fairfax to the blush a little, thinking of his years as a Grub Street hack, often translating dirty French and Italian books into dirty English ones.) Sir Edward wanted someone to catalogue and put in order a vast and eclectic collection that he had inherited from his recently deceased father—several thousand volumes, as well as maps, prints, coins, curios, papers, and correspondence. The someone would receive a secretary's salary and live with the family while the task was in progress. An accessible antiquarian, a biddable bookworm, was needed.

And so, it seemed Fairfax's luck had held after all! A

short interview with the baronet at his London apartments—
Sir Edward was in town for a few weeks on legal business—
and the bargain was struck. Fairfax, who had been living in
an attic lodging by St. Paul's in hopes of picking up some
hack work from the booksellers thereabout, paid his last
week's rent with his last shillings, packed his life-containing
trunk, and joined Sir Edward at the Bull in Bishopsgate
Street. They were to travel in easy stages by hired post
chaise, up the Great North Road to Stamford; Cheyney Hall
lay within a few miles of that elegant market town. They had
broken the journey overnight at Royston, and now were
bowling along in good time in the windy autumn morning,
brittle torrents of leaves swirling and racing about their red-
rimmed wheels, and hoping to reach their destination before
dinner.

"Ah, it'll be sweet to see my little chicks again," Sir Edward said. "Not so little now, mind—I fear I'll find them
grown again after a mere month. Letitia is just turned seventeen, Amelia fifteen. Aye me, they'll be taking wing all
too soon. They've plagued me, in every letter, to be allowed
to go to the Assembly in Stamford this week. 'Tis a genteel
occasion, right enough, and I daresay fitting for their first
out. But I see it as—well, the stage from which there is no
turning back." He shrugged ruefully. "A fond father's folly.
Well, they are excellent girls, pretty as paint, and with good
heads on their shoulders. I don't believe in women being
brought up to nothing but ignorance and coquetry."

Fairfax was finding the baronet an interesting mixture.
Sir Edward was vigorous and straightforward and thor-
oughly conventional in many of his ways—yet he was no
boor. His ruddy English face, with strong nose and pugna-
cious jaw, was enlivened by gray, intelligent, faintly melancholy eyes.

"The young ladies have had instruction?"

"Aye, they've been well taught—they have French and
music and so forth; and then they have instructed themselves—what with their grandfather's library, and his in-

quiring spirit too. They were sore grieved when he died—always lived at Cheyney with him, you see. As did I, from the day I was wed. By the time he died, my father was elderly, and wrapped up in his books, and I was pretty much the master in all but name. A common enough arrangement in the old families. And, of course, I was sore grieved too . . . but I think you are sufficiently a man of the world, Fairfax, to understand that I was also a mite relieved. I was proud to be old Sir Jemmy's son—but not that alone, forever. At two-and-forty, the title 'young master' doesn't sit too well on your shoulders, you know; to be plain, it itches like a drover's blanket. Mind, I've no thought of breaking up my father's collection, nor selling any part. 'Tis only that I'm no scholar, and don't know my way about it—nor did anyone but he, in truth. We used to say he lived in it like a badger in his sett, and not even the housekeeper dared disturb the diggings."

"I hope I shall do justice to it," Fairfax said, very humble—and fascinated. He had actually had dreams of being let loose in such a library, and woken full of disappointed longing. God's life, he thought, what does *that* say about me . . . ? "And the Assembly, Sir Edward—shall you relent?"

"Ha! They know full well I will, little minxes," Sir Edward said with a smile of great tenderness. "Ah, excellent, we're coming to Huntingdon. I've the devil's own thirst, and my guts are yawning. We'll get good victualing at the Bridge. Then fresh horses, and on"—he slapped his great knee—"to home and hearth. God saving, of course, that we don't find ourselves staring into a highwayman's pistols at the foot of Alconbury Hill." He gave his great trumpeting laugh again.

Fairfax laughed too; then wondered why he should think of the old proverb, He laughs ill who laughs himself to death . . .

*   *   *

The yard of the Bridge at Huntingdon was as busy as befitted a coaching house on the Great North Road: sleek horses being led out to exercise from the stables; lathered horses being taken from the shafts of post chaises; farmers chewing the fat and doing a little business over the backboards of their carts; grooms and postboys hurrying across the cobbles with clomping boots on their feet, leather tackle festooned about their necks, and loud horsy argon on their lips. "Wisp her over, Sam—gently, she's a miller." "This drag's took a scrape—that lame hand over there feather-edged it on the bridge." "Sharp on the ribbons, that's why."

Then, more comprehensible, the innkeeper welcoming Sir Edward and adding, as he wiped his hands on his apron, "You drove up from the South road, sir?"

"Aye, Royston was our last stage. Why?"

"Oh, I was wondering, if you'd come from the north, whether you'd seen aught of the *Stamford Flyer* on the way. The public coach, you know, sir, and regular as a coach may be; we expected it here twenty minutes ago."

"The *Flyer*, eh? Usually keeps good time," Sir Edward said, surprised. "Mind, we found some heavy going in the hollows this morning, even driving post."

"Aye, just what I thought, sir—this late rain—it must be the state of the road." The innkeeper glanced with a frown at the inn-yard gate. "Not like the *Flyer*, though . . . Well, sirs, how can I serve you?"

Sir Edward bespoke a private eating room, ordering wine, veal and ham pie, and beef patties.

"It will stay our stomachs till dinner," he said, clapping his hands with relish. "I keep a good table at Cheyney, Fairfax, and you must take advantage of it—you're as thin as a rasher of wind."

A man of erratic appetite, Fairfax wondered how he would keep up. He felt like a frail-stemmed glass beside the sturdy Toby jug of Sir Edward.

Crossing the yard, they passed a man holding a saddle horse by the bridle, and talking to a groom.

"She seems to favor that foot—something amiss with the shoeing, perhaps," the man was saying tentatively.

Sir Edward, who Fairfax already knew was a passionate expert on the subject of horseflesh, turned at once and deftly lifted the horse's foot onto his knee, examining the shoe with keen eyes. "By your leave . . . Why, man, it's the most mob-handed shoeing I ever saw in my life! The nails are half out, don't you see?"

"I had not observed it." The man was plainly, soberly dressed, the broadcloth coat and worsted stockings suggesting a small tradesman or farmer: spare, square-shouldered, a little gaunt, he wore his own grizzled hair tied severely back and had the most intensely blue and penetrating eyes Fairfax had ever seen.

"I don't know how you could miss it," Sir Edward said in his bluff way, releasing the horse's foot. "But you'd do best to change your blacksmith, for whoever did this isn't worth his hire."

The baronet was plainly a man accustomed to a certain deference. Just as plainly, the stranger was a man who did not readily give it.

"I seldom visit the same smith twice," he said. "I am about the country a good deal, traveling on the Lord's business. The shoeing of my horse is a small matter."

"Not to the horse it ain't." Sir Edward gave the man a thorough look. "What, you're a parson, sir, are you?"

"I have not been ordained," the man said in the same pale, informative, unaccommodating tone. "I have been called by my God to carry the bread of His Word to those famished for it, wherever they may be."

Sir Edward's great head went up—very like a shying horse, Fairfax thought. "A Methody." The baronet's tone said everything, and he was about to stump past into the inn when the man spoke again.

"I find no disgrace in the term, sir."

"Oh, plainly, my good fellow, plainly. Come, Fairfax,"

Sir Edward said, shaking his head and chuckling, "else we'll be preached to death before we get our victuals."

Fairfax followed, feeling—as his employer did not seem to feel—the uncompromising stare of the homespun man following them into the inn.

"You do not approve of Mr. Wesley and his works?" Fairfax said, as a cloth was laid for them in a snug paneled supper room with low beams and a sulky fire.

"I do not. And neither can any rational, sensible man who wishes to preserve the property, integrity, and peace of the country. " Sir Edward took a deep draft of his pint of wine. "What is this Methodism, after all? A set of wild preachers, constituted as such only by the say-so of fanatics and not by any established church, roaming among the poor and the impressionable and turning their wits with raving enthusiasm, till they think in their absurd pride they are the first and only creatures ever to be Christian. 'Tis a very ill meddling, sir, very ill."

"Yet Mr. Wesley is quite a Tory, they say—enjoins strict submission to the social order, humility, industry. The things of the next world concern him, not this . . . And often his people are bringing religion to places, in remote spots and mines and seaports, where there simply are no churches."

Sir Edward studied Fairfax with a shrewd look. "Ho, now *you* are trying to convert me."

"Not at all," Fairfax said, smiling. "I count myself upon the rational side. And much of Methodism repels me, as overheated superstition and emotionalism . . . Yet there must be some need for it. The poorer people, especially, seem to thirst for what it offers."

"There you have it precisely—the essential germ of danger and sedition in it. For what is it planting in these folks' minds? The notion that the Church has failed them. Duly established society—parish and parson—has nothing for them. So they reject them. What next? Landlord, government, king? I wonder. I say, Fairfax, stand the door ajar, will you? This fire's smoking like the devil's dunghill."

As Fairfax did so, in the common dining room beyond he noticed the Methodist preacher sitting down at a plain board close by, and quietly asking for bread and cheese.

"By the by, Fairfax," Sir Edward said, refilling his glass, "I can't swear to this, but I fancy there may be some rather broad material among my father's collections. He really did take all knowledge for his province, as Bacon has it, and there may well be engravings or volumes of a rather, hum, pagan character. I thought I'd mention it, while we're on the subject of morality . . . Ah, here comes our provender. Leave the door, man, this fire's smeeching. Not that I see you as a prig, Fairfax, in the least. After all, weren't you telling me your mother was a Frenchwoman?" Sir Edward chuckled.

"She was indeed. And the very fact was sufficient to make people think her like to be immoral, when she first came to England. After all, to anything dubious or indecent we tag on the word *French*—yet in France they do the same with us. You have doubtless heard of the 'English vice,' and of *copotes anglaises . . .*"

Sir Edward was rumbling with laughter as he ate. "So, sin is always what the other fellow is up to, eh?"

At the word *sin* Fairfax saw the preacher in the next room lift his head from his frugal meal like a dog alerted by its name.

"Well," Fairfax said, "some would say sin is absolute."

"Both—such as yon fellow with the half-lame horse, you mean? Oh, but 'tis a ranting tinker's faith they preach, and a damned intrusive one, poking into the privacy of men's souls. The state of my soul is a matter for me and my Maker. And I hope when the time comes we may settle the account like gentlemen, without bawling the business out in a farm-yard prayerfest with hysterical women fainting on all sides. All I ask of religion is that it should not be *vulgar*."

It was a rational, worldly, aristocratic attitude often met with in people of Sir Edward's class. Fairfax had even known eminent divines who shared it. As an admirer of

Voltaire and a freethinker, Fairfax himself privately took enlightenment a step further . . . And yet there was a dark and melancholic side to him that saw the allure in the hellfire conviction, the black-and-white fervor, of men like the Methodist preacher—who was now standing in the doorway of the supper room, regarding the occupants with his compellingly pale eyes.

" 'What is truth? said jesting Pilate; and would not stay for an answer,' " he said. He had a singularly beautiful and musical voice, deep and resonant with a slight edge of sadness. Fairfax could imagine its effect at an outdoor field preaching.

"Ah!" Sir Edward sat back good-humoredly, glass to his lips, regarding the neat slight figure much as his ancestors might have regarded a motleyed jester capering up to divert them. "Bacon again. Our minds run parallel, my friend, even if they cannot meet. Will you drink a glass with us?"

The preacher shook his head minutely. "I don't touch it, sir."

"No. Scripture, I suppose. But then doesn't Scripture say something about taking a little wine for thy stomach's sake?"

"I cannot be provoked, sir, by such trifling. My feet are set too firm upon the rock of salvation for that. I mean no disrespect, but I cannot sit by and hear a man speak jestingly of holy things." The preacher pointed a steady finger at the baronet. "Out of very concern for *your* immortal soul, I cannot."

Sir Edward's bushy eyebrows rose. "My eternal soul ain't your business, my good man. But this rock, now, with your feet so firmly set upon it, and so forth—how do you *know* this, might I ask? This is what perplexes me about your sort, Mr. Preacher. You sincerely believe that you are utterly in the right of it—always, world without end? Such assurance! Almost like pride, is it not? And after all, what is to separate you from any mountebank at the fair who says that his miraculous elixir will cure everything from toothache to the pox?"

Sir Edward was amusing himself; that the preacher knew it was plainly written on his face, but he spoke temperately. "All men's souls are my concern, sir. And just now I tremble for yours. I see the flames licking about it."

"I'm conscious of no heat, Mr. Preacher." But there was vexation in Sir Edward's laugh.

"I have a name, sir; it is Henry Griggs."

"Well, Henry Griggs, mine is Sir Edward Nugent, of Cheyney Hall, Northamptonshire. I don't know where you intend pitching your next prayerfest, but let me advise you I will not allow it on my land, and as a magistrate I shall not look kindly on such gatherings either."

Henry Griggs barely inclined his head, and said composedly, "I have a standing invitation from the Methodist society here at Huntingdon to speak, and to wreak a revival of the Spirit here, if the Lord wills. We meet only in peace and brotherhood, sir, to be washed in the blood of the Lamb. None come to harm; many come to good, You might come to good yourself, Sir Edward Nugent."

"An entertaining impudence. But one can have enough of it." Sir Edward looked suddenly bored, and helped himself to the last pie. "Good day, Mr. Preacher."

Henry Griggs seemed about to correct him again, but with another passionless, penetrating stare, went away.

"You meant it?" Fairfax said.

"Certainly. And I know that Lord Burghley of Burghley House, who is the most considerable man in the district, and chairman of the justices, is no friend to our Mr. Griggs and his like either. Why, man, never tell me he's won you over?"

"No, but I should be interested to hear such a man preach, as an experience."

"You're like my father," Sir Edward grunted, "interested, in everything. A man should cultivate a little dull indifference, Fairfax, to give him ballast. Well, let the good burghers of Huntingdon endure the fellow's ravings." Sir

Edward tossed a handful of coins down. "Come, Fairfax—why, man, you've hardly ate a morsel—we'll go see if the horses have been changed."

The post chaise, elegant in yellow and black, with a pair of fresh-groomed horses stamping in the shafts, stood ready in the yard. There too was the innkeeper, still fretting over the lateness of the *Stamford Flyer*.

"'Tis mighty unlike it. Dear me. Here's a gentleman booked an inside seat, and needs to be in Baldock this evening."

He pointed to a testy old clergyman leaning on a silver-topped stick, who patted his vast powdered wig pettishly and grumbled: "I am to officiate at a funeral. Two children, of *very* good family. If I do not appear, 'twill likely be conducted by some wretch of a curate with dirt under his nails: hardly fitting. I shall take this up with the coach proprietors, upon my word I shall, and my bishop shall hear of it."

"Coach must have foundered," Sir Edward said as the yellow-jacketed postilion mounted the lead horse, and he and Fairfax stepped into the post chaise. "Let's hope there's no one hurt."

The horses were very fresh, and as most postilions drove at a gallop, they were soon rattling along at a speed that made Fairfax wish he had eaten even more sparingly of the rich pie than he had. But a check soon came to their progress in the shape of Alconbury Hill, a notoriously hard climb for wheeled traffic of all kinds. As the coach strained and lurched up the ascent, Fairfax commented on the singularity of such a considerable hill occurring in such an expanse of flatness.

"'Twas a little provoking of Providence," agreed Sir Edward. "We are on the edge of the fen country here, which is no more hilly than a bowling green. And there are surprising dense woods down about Stangate Hole, before we get to Stilton, which have always been mighty convenient for our friends of the mask-and-pistol persuasion . . . Whoa, down we go. Don't looks so green, Fairfax, we'll soon be on level going again."

The coach bucketed down the descent with an almighty rattling of the axles and swingle bars, the glasses and the coach lamps; only the rattling of Fairfax's teeth in his head seemed louder. A long queasy swaying of the whole vehicle from one side to the other, like the lashing of a great tail, indicated that they had reached the bottom. Fairfax settled his hat on his head and swallowed down something unpleasant in his throat. Level going, thank heaven.

They had about five minutes of it before the coach lurched again—but this time because the postilion had pulled up the horses sharp, with a curious shout audible over the noise of hoofs and wheels. Swearing, Sir Edward pulled down the glass and started to bellow out to him.

"What the devil are we stopping for—"

Fairfax silenced him with a hand on his arm. Through the other window, over at the right-hand side of the empty road, he had seen what the postilion had seen. And even before the details had imprinted themselves on his mind, he hoped that he would never see a worse sight.

Two

The stretch of straight level road on which they had been traveling was lined on the left side by oak trees, outposts of the woods that lay in smoke-colored folds all about the near distance. On the right, the verge of the road fell away among gorse and bramble into a shallow ditch, with a steeper bank rising on the other side to a strip of plowed field and then more woods, close and dark.

There, with its far side wheels in the ditch so that the whole coach lay at a forty-five-degree angle, was the *Stamford Flyer*. The name of the coach was visible, painted in curlicue on the door panel that stood open on the near side. The horses were still in the traces, the front pair standing square on the verge, with the leader even calm enough to be nibbling grass, the rear pair half in the ditch, lathered and agitated and whinnying shrilly at the sight of the post chaise and the two men hurrying over.

But it was not the plight of the horses that chiefly concerned Fairfax and his employer. It was the bodies.

One lay on the edge of the ditch directly behind the tilted roof of the coach, with one booted foot still on the roof rail; an outside passenger, Fairfax thought. The other was the coachman, slumped across the driving seat and practically upside down, though the reins were still gathered up under his lifeless arms.

Fairfax stared down at the man sprawled by the ditch. His head spun and he felt sick.

"Does he live?" breathed Sir Edward beside him. "Oh— dear God."

Fairfax turned away. The man had been shot in the face, the ball entering the cheek and making havoc. The dark hair was matted to the roots with blood. With his arms spread wide and his smashed face he was more like a scarecrow than a human being.

"Devilish," Sir Edward grunted, turning away too. "Devilish work . . . Don't look, boy," he said to the postilion who had joined them, whey-faced. "Free those poor beasts from the traces—I doubt they'll bolt. Great God, are there any inside . . . ?"

Fairfax was already scrambling up the tilted step of the coach to look in the interior. He saw the dashes of blood on the glass in the open door first. Then the figure slumped across the horsehair seat, its head lolling at an impossible angle in the corner of the bodywork. No featureless mess this time: the man's face—white, pinched, and astonished— was unmarked beneath a powdered bagwig, with steel spectacles perched a little askew on the nose. Just below was the bloody horror—he had been shot in the throat. On the seat beside him was a carved wooden ear trumpet, and at his feet a small iron-clasped strongbox, open and empty.

There was no need to touch him: only death had that frozen stillness.

"Fairfax"!" Sir Edward's voice. "Help me—the coachman, I think he still lives . . ."

With trembling difficulty, the two of them clambered up on the footboard and lifted the coachman from the seat. The postilion, who had swiftly cut the coach horses from the traces with a sharp penknife, reached up from below and took his feet. The coachman was a big man, dressed in heavy boots and a cumbrous greatcoat. Fairfax felt the muscles in his arms would snap in the struggle to get the man down gently. But they managed it, and laid him on the grass.

The coachman's eyelids were fluttering. Sir Edward took off the man's broad hat, put a hesitant hand toward the bloodied lock of grizzled hair that covered his left temple, then withdrew it. Shot in the head, Fairfax thought. But might the ball have merely winged him, not completed its killing flight?

"We should send for a surgeon," Fairfax said. "The man inside is dead, but there may be hope here . . . What's the nearest town? Huntingdon?"

"Yes—yes, that would be best." Sir Edward addressed the postilion. "Fas as you can back to Huntingdon, my boy. Tell them at the inn what's happened, and have them find a surgeon for this man. Then there's these other poor wretches . . . they cannot lie here . . . Bespeak a cart or a wagon of some sort too, boy; tell them Sir Edward Nugent will bear the change. Ride the lead horse from the chaise, that will be quickest. Off, now."

As the postilion galloped away, Fairfax bent close to the weathered face of the coachman, whose lips were faintly moving.

"Hod up, my friend. Help's coming. Can you speak?"

The coachman's chest rose laboriously. He gave a long, faint groan.

"Here . . ." Sir Edward fumbled in his pocket and brought out his brandy flask. "Put a little to his lips."

Before Fairfax could do so the coachman's eyes opened fully. They moved with a terrible snaillike slowness from one face to the other. A sigh came from his throat, becoming a word.

"High . . . wayman . . ." He could only give it the faintest articulation. Fairfax bent closer.

"We'll have the rogue," Sir Edward said. "Never fear, friend, he'll swing."

Forgetting himself, Fairfax made an impatient hushing motion. The coachman was speaking again.

"Tried . . . drive straight on . . . tried . . ." With sudden agitation he made an effort to turn his head in the direction of the crashed coach. "Never upset before . . . never . . . all my years . . ."

"Rest easy. You're not to blame." Fairfax unstoppered the flask and trickled a little brandy onto the coachman's lips. It ran down his chin. No response from the lips. Nor, Fairfax saw now, from the eyes, which in turning toward the coach had stilled, glazed, died.

Fairfax sat back on his haunches. A time for a prayer. But it should have come unbidden; instead the doubt and skepticism of his nature entangled and silenced him. It was Sir Edward who supplied it, simply.

"God have mercy on his soul." With a swift unsentimental motion the baronet closed the empty eyes and stood up. "Three innocent lives. Snuffed out for gain. Our man has excelled himself this time. Well, well."

"You think this is the work of the man you spoke of earlier?"

"No doubt of it. This is his haunt. Not for long, though. He shall be caught and dispatched to hell where he belongs. I shall personally double the price on his head."

"Yet he has never used such brutality before."

"He has now. Unless you think these poor creatures are dressmakers' dummies, hey, Fairfax?"

Fairfax glanced up; occupied with his thoughts, he had not realized quite how angry and disgusted Sir Edward was.

"The crime is unspeakable," Fairfax said. "I was just wondering at the manner of it. It would seem the coachman tried to drive on when accosted by the robber—perhaps to ride him down. Brave if foolhardy. And the robber stopped the coach in the directest manner—shot the coachman in his seat. Lacking direction, the coach tipped into the ditch. And then . . ."

"Then the brute murdered the passengers. One outside, one in. Simple and beastly enough."

"Yes . . . yet I wonder if there was more than one brute. Such a man would usually be armed with a brace of pistols,

I understand, primed and loaded so that he would get one shot from each if needed. Yet here are three people shot."

"An accomplice, think you? Or a gang? But this fellow's known for plying his trade quite alone."

Fairfax nodded. "Of course he might have had more than a brace of pistols about him, though it's unlikely."

"More probable that he primed and reloaded after the first two shots. Killed the coachman and the outside passenger—the poor fellow probably tried to make a bolt for it when the coach was upset—then proceeded to deal with the man inside at his leisure. Ecod, 'tis all as fish-blooded and efficient as you like."

Sir Edward's summary was very much how Fairfax saw these events, yet still something about the utter ruthless violence of the scene perplexed him.

"The gentleman inside carried a strongbox, which has been emptied," he said. "Perhaps he was the highwayman's main quarry."

"Which means the villain knew that gentleman would be riding the *Flyer* today. No great mystery there; these fellows make it their business to get such information from the inns and posting houses. They skulk about on their own account, or they pump ostlers and chambermaids and such. 'Tis not unheard of for innkeepers themselves to be in league with these fellows, taking a share of the profits. Ah, but the *FLyer* starts from the George at Stamford, one of the principal establishments of the country. The innkeeper there is a man of substance and unimpeachable character—indeed, I fancy he is part proprietor of the *Flyer*." Sir Edward put out a peremptory hand for the brandy flask and took a swig. "Good God, what a horror. Those poor beasts hardly know where they are."

With great address the postilion had managed to tether the coach horses by their cut traces to a fence post, but they showed no sign of wanting to go anywhere. They huddled together, shivering, stamping, scenting death. The now solitary horse in the shafts of the post chaise scented it too: it tossed its head and rolled its eyes at its brethren across the road.

"It is hard to tell what he meant," Fairfax said, still pondering. "He said 'highwayman'—or it might have been 'highwaymen.' The sound is much alike, even when clearly spoken. A puzzle . . . Well, I suppose these woods would provide cover for a dozen such, at any rate."

"Monks Wood, to the east there, covers scores of acres alone. Whose the land, I don't know: maybe Fitzwilliam. A thorough combing, by a great many armed men, might flush out a gallows bird or two—if such a body could ever be raised, and if they gave absolutely no hint of their approach. Unlikely at best."

"Perhaps whatever was taken from that strongbox will furnish the best clue," Fairfax said, accepting the proffered brandy flask. "The culprit will have to spend or dispose of it at some time."

"Aye, there's that—not that these villains don't have their own set of fences and brokers. Well, there may be something that's identifiable. Depends who these poor souls are. Their names will be recorded at the inn booking office in Stamford."

"The *Flyer*'s destination is London?"

"Aye—it takes in Huntingdon, but then goes by way of Biggleswade and Hatfield—the true Great North Road, rather than the old North Road we came by. More towns, so more fares to be had that way, I suppose. I've ridden the *Flyer* myself, with my girls . . ." Sir Edward visibly shuddered. "There are families awaiting the arrival of these murdered wretches even now: wives, children . . . I mean to make this my business, Fairfax, as a magistrate and as a fellow mortal. There is no forgetting such a sight."

"Amen to that," Fairfax said soberly. He had seen death before, but the bleak and grisly end that these people had met, on an empty high road of scuttering leaves and staring sky, was uniquely chilling.

There came hoofbeats from the road to the south, but it

was not the help they awaited: instead, a string of three packhorse riders, who pulled up at the site with all the shock and dismay of the first discoverers. But they were on their way to Stamford, so Sir Edward charged them with taking the news of the disaster to the George Inn there, the *Flyer*'s home port.

"The bodies had best be carried to Stamford for now," Sir Edward said when the riders had gone. "That's where they set out from. We can find out their names there, and identify them. There will have to be an inquest, of course. Though 'tis a plain and simple case enough: murder, no less."

Plain enough, Fairfax thought, but simple? He wasn't sure. He began studying the ground round about the crashed coach, trying to reconstruct the incident in his mind.

The assailant, or assailants, must have known the time when the coach would be due here—common knowledge enough—and waited among the trees for its approach. Then, out into the road—mounted, of course, for highway robbers always were, as opposed to the footpads who lurked about the outskirts of towns—a shouted challenge, pistols at the ready. The coachman's last words suggested that he had tried to drive on, courageously or stubbornly. Looking at the south road ahead, with its steep ascent to Alconbury Hill in the distance, Fairfax saw that that had been more foolish than either. His progress would soon have been slowed by the incline, certainly enough for a determined mounted man to have swiftly caught up.

It was a purely theoretical point, anyhow, because the coachman had met a very determined adversary indeed—one who had shot him without hesitation.

Fairfax conned the surface of the road, which was quite soft and muddy a this low point. But it was just a confusion of wheel ruts and hoofprints, including no doubt those of their own post chaise. He had heard tales from men who had been in the American colonies of Red Indians who could read the ground at their feet like a book, but the gift was beyond him.

So, with the coachman shot, and the coach horses no doubt in a panic, the vehicle itself had swerved and tipped into the ditch, its far-side wheels wedging there, the horses unable to go on . . . And the outside passengers? It would seem there was only one: the fellow who lay at the edge of the ditch. A youngish man, dressed in a long greatcoat and muffler, apt enough for outside traveling, which was a notoriously cold business. Dangerous too, as one had simply to cling on to the coach roof as best one could throughout the jolting, pitching journey. Not that the traveler could have anticipated such mortal danger as this . . . So, had he been thrown from the roof as the coach tipped into the ditch, and been shot where he fell? Or had he clung on, and then tried to make an escape, as Sir Edward suggested? Certainly it seemed likely that he and the coachman had been dispatched first, and then the robber or robbers had approached the coach door. If there was only one, that must have been when he primed and reloaded his pistols—cool and levelheaded indeed. After all, there were plenty of travelers who went armed themselves, as a precaution against just such an attack, and who knew what might await the criminal inside the coach? Unless, of course, he had precise knowledge of that very fact. And as for cool and levelheaded, the whole undertaking merited those words. Cool, levelheaded—and pitiless.

Taking a deep breath, Fairfax climbed up again to look in at the coach door. With the far-side window pressed against the bank of the ditch, it was quite dim inside, which would explain why, the first time, he had not spotted the object tucked into the dead man's right palm.

It was a flintlock pistol, of the sort called a "man-stopper": small enough to be carried in the pocket, and in fact ideal for a man traveling with valuables. Fairfax himself had carried a pair like this on his Grand Tour of the Continent as a young man, though he had never had to use them. But what of this man? Had he perhaps managed a shot . . . ?

"Sir Edward—look here, if you will."

The baronet thrust his great head into the coach. "God in heaven, the poor fellow . . . I've seen enough blood, Fairfax—let us leave it until these bodies can be carried away decently."

"But look at this. He was armed." Fairfax lifted the pistol from the stiff curled hand.

"Think you he winged our man? God, I hope so. He'll be injured if so, losing blood; he'll have to seek out a doctor. 'Tis our best hope."

Fairfax, holding the pistol up to the light, shook his head. "This has not been fired. See? Primed and loaded—powder in the pan. But he did not fire." He laid the pistol down on the seat, then reached for the dead man's left hand, which was tucked at an angle in his breast. "And here, within the pocket, I believe we will find the other . . . Just so." The handle of the companion pistol protruded from the breast pocket of the man's snuff brown coat. Drawing it out was difficult . . . "Yes," said Fairfax finally.

"Yes what, damn it?"

"I once carried such a pair of pistols myself. Mighty convenient except for this—the exposed lock and trigger. Liable to snag in the lining of your pocket when you draw them out. No great matter, except—"

"Except when someone is pointing a pistol at you, and every instant is vital," said Sir Edward, shaking his head. "Poor fellow. I trust it was over quick. Come, Fairfax. The matter is plain enough."

Fairfax climbed out. But there was something more he wanted to examine: the rumble, at the rear of the coach, where the passengers' luggage was stored. It was empty.

"Probably stolen too, if there was any," Sir Edward said. "And the gentleman inside would no doubt wish to keep that strongbox close by him."

Fairfax nodded thoughtfully. "It would be curious for a man of substance, as he appears to have been, to have no baggage at all. Of course, it depends where he was going—which we can find out at the Stamford coach office. Probably a record of luggage too . . ." He raised his head: the sound of wheels on the south road.

Their postilion was returning, riding alongside a light cart driven by a groom. Behind them came a man on horse-back.

The groom swept off his hat, very hushed and respectful, solemnly presenting the compliments of the innkeeper at Huntingdon, and saying that his master had placed him entirely at their disposal for this terrible occasion. "Terrible," he repeated, his eyes ghoulishly straying to the wrecked coach, "terrible . . ." Probably the whole staff of the inn were eagerly depending on him for the scarifying details.

"Dr. Tuplin," Sir Edward said to the mounted man, who had already got down and was hurrying over to the coach-man, "I fear it's too late—we find no signs of life. All three slaughtered . . ."

Without comment the doctor, a fair, stooping man past thirty, with his own hair tied in a simple queue, bent to examine the coachman then passed swiftly to the man by the ditch. Finally he leaped up into the coach. He soon emerged, wiping his hands on a handkerchief, a kind of pained abstraction on his lined face.

"Dr. Tuplin," Sir Edward said in introduction to Fairfax. "A Stamford man—fine physician."

"I might deserve your tribute if I could revive these poor souls," Dr. Tuplin said with a wan smile. "But I am afraid that is beyond any man's power. It was quite by chance I was in Huntingdon today, and had stabled my horse at the inn there. I am surgeon to all the jails, lockups, and work-houses hereabout, and this week Huntingdon was the scene of my delightful duty." In Tuplin's words and his expression Fairfax caught a familiar echo—the hollowness of a disappointed man. "Well, the best I can tell you is that these people can have suffered but little. The execution was swift and sure."

"The coachman lived a few minutes after we found him,"

Sir Edward said. "Long enough to tell us it was that villain we all seek."

"Our predatory friend has certainly excelled himself," Dr. Tuplin said, shaking his head at Sir Edward's proffered flask. "I'm no army surgeon, and have little experience of these matters, but it would seem that whoever wielded the pistols meant quite earnestly to kill." He frowned. "The man in the coach I believe I know vaguely . . . yet I am not certain. Death soon transforms. I can examine them more closely and certify the deaths if they are conveyed to a better place. Their bodies, I mean," he said with that same hollow look, meeting Fairfax's eye. "Their souls, naturally, have already made the journey."

"I thought to have them brought to Stamford, where they set out," Sir Edward said. "There can be no objection, I suppose? I am a magistrate for the borough, if not for this forsaken spot of ground."

"I can think of no better direction," the doctor agreed. Again he glanced over at the coach. "Strange, I swear there is something familiar about that gentleman . . . Well, no matter. I'm ready to bear a hand in lifting them into the cart. I have quite as much to do with the dead as the living—as do most of us sawbones, if we would but admit it."

It was soon done, the bodies being laid in the bed of the cart as decently as their condition allowed, and covered with some sacking the groom had brought for the purpose. The empty strongbox was placed there too. The resourceful postilion hitched the coach horses to the back of the post chaise; and thus the strange procession—cart, post chaise, and the doctor on horseback—made its way up the Great North Road. The packhorse men must have passed the news at Stilton, the next posting stage, for people came crowding out of the famous Bell Inn to stare at the impromptu cortege; likewise at Wansford, the next stop; and when at last they came in the darkening afternoon to St. Martin's, the outlying parish of the town of Stamford, people were standing expectantly outside cottage doors, many bareheaded. A pack of ragged boys came running alongside the cart, trying to peep in, undeterred by the groom's cutting about him with his whip.

Fairfax had never been to Stamford, but had heard much of its architectural and social elegance, which made it a favorite town residence for the gentry of the region. The prospect as they came down High Street St. Martin's, with ahead the bridge arching the river and leading to a graceful sweep of gray stone gables and soaring spires, was a handsome one—quite as fine as Oxford, he thought. Another time he would have given it close attention.

But any impression could only be faint compared with that made by the bodies in the cart. Somehow they seemed even more pathetic, laid and covered thus, than they had looked at the scene of the killings. There, something of themselves remained; now they were enlisted in the anonymous ranks of the dead.

The George at Stamford was one of the great inns of England. It announced itself with a great timber sign that stretched right across the street from roof to roof like an arch—or a gallows. Another crowd of people was gathered at the wide coach gate of the inn. This was the place from which the *Flyer* had set out on its doomed journey.

The procession turned into the yard. Almost at once a plump, pug-nosed, bustling man, his eyes round with alarm, was at the post chaise window.

"Sir Edward," he stammered, opening the carriage door, "I hardly know what to think. Some fellows came riding in with the most dreadful intelligence, but I cannot believe—"

"'Tis true enough, I'm afraid, Quigley. The *Flyer* has been held up, and is foundered." Sir Edward stepped down and addressed the fluttering man sternly. "You must compose yourself, my friend. The passengers are killed, and the coachman. 'Tis done. But we shall have this brute at last, Quigley, my word on it. This will be his last outrage."

Mr. Quigley, whom Fairfax guessed to be the innkeeper of the George, stared and swallowed and took a deep breath.

Then he nodded and walked slowly over to the cart and looked in.

When he returned his round comfortable face was ashen.

"Never in my worst dreams," he said huskily. "Safe and convenient traveling—that's how we have always advertised the *Flyer*. My partner in London once spoke of placing a guard on the coach, but it's an extravagance for a modest country operation . . . My poor coachman! A sterling fellow—I cannot believe it . . ."

"Has he been long in your service?"

"Ten years. He boards here at the George. Crabbe is his name, Charles Crabbe. Such a sturdy fellow, some other coach proprietors have tried to poach him away from me. Poor Crabbe . . ."

"Has he family?"

"No—no, thank heaven, a bachelor. Coaching was all his life. It was his boast that he had never had an upset, and true enough."

"He lived long enough to speak to us," Fairfax said, "and mentioned a highwayman, or men. Also something about trying to drive on . . . ?"

Mr. Quigley plucked at his lip. "That's likely enough. He used to be mighty fierce on the subject of this rogue who's plaguing the roads—said that if ever he saw him he would ply his whip and drive the scoundrel down in the road."

Sir Edward nodded. "The scoundrel, alas, was too sharp for him. I'm afraid your coach lies in a ditch, Quigley, down by Stangate Hole, and there must be some damage."

With an anguished shrug, and evident sincerity, the innkeeper said, "What's that beside innocent lives?"

Dr. Tuplin was there. "A place for laying-out is needed," he said, "and I doubt, Mr. Quigley, your patrons would relish such guests under your roof. I would suggest the Cross Keys—it is just round the corner in Church Street, and the publican there does undertaking; he has a room for the purpose." The publican-undertaker was not an uncommon figure in country towns. "I shall examine the bodies, and make an inventory of their clothes and possessions for submission to the coroner."

"Very well, Tuplin," Sir Edward said. "I leave it in your hands. Quigley, we shall need to know who these poor wretches were. You don't recollect who boarded the *Flyer* this morning?"

"I wasn't on hand when she loaded," the innkeeper said. "And I don't generally take down the bookings myself. Old Jacob has the charge of that. Used to be my head ostler till he got the screws in the back. We'll go see him. He writes a fair hand, and he's as honest a man as ever trod leather, so I find him some light work that way . . ."

Talking agitatedly, Mr. Quigley led them inside. Fairfax noticed twin coffee rooms for coach passengers, one with "York" inscribed above the door, the other "London." In each there was an urgent babble of talk, and pale expectant faces swiveled as they passed.

Old Jacob turned out to be a very old man indeed, so bent that the line of his shoulders came above his head, and the seat of his breeches below his knees. The snug office in which they found him, with a brass-railed counter and a high-backed chair, and a good fire burning, reflected well on Mr. Quigley's kindness as an employer, Fairfax thought. Old Jacob was also a little deaf, but his mind and his handwriting were clear enough.

"I have it to hand, sir—all as plain as you like." He opened the large ledger on the counter by tottering to one end of it and with both hands heaving at it like the hatch of a cellar. "Entered for the *Flyer*, departing for London at seven o'clock in the morning, Tuesday, the sixth of October 1761: outside passengers one, inside passengers two . . ."

"Two?" Fairfax said.

"One was a short stage, mebbe, and got down earlier," Mr. Quigley said, drawing the ledger toward him and reading his servant's careful script. "Inside, Mr. Twelvetree, for Huntingdon, paid fifteen shillings, to board the coach at the

Haycock, Wansford . . ." The innkeeper's voice grew faint. "Twelvetree . . ."

"What's amiss, sir?" Old Jacob, who had evidently not heard about the murders, quavered. "Not upset, is she? I heard the grooms making a to-do outside.

"Aye, upset," Sir Edward said, "a bad business. Twelvetree, eh? That would explain the strongbox. My Lord, Nicholas Twelvetree . . ."

"He is known to you?" Fairfax said

"I know of him. Most folk around here do, at least by name: keeps himself to himself in the main. Kept, I should say. Poor wretch." Sir Edward's look, though, was as much wry as sorrowful. "He is a banker—damn it, was. One of the warmest men in the town. When I say warm, I mean only in the sense of wealthy. No one ever called him warm in the other way, I think. Well, his people had better be told at once."

"He has family?" Fairfax said.

"Not to speak of. I was thinking of the bank people. But what's this about boarding at Wansford?"

"Sir, the fare was paid at this office," Jacob said, running a proprietary finger down the columns, "on the fourth of the month. 'Twas a clerk came in to book it, I seem to think. But the gentleman was to board at Wansford, the next stop down."

"That's rum," Sir Edward said. "Twelvetree hardly stirred abroad from his house, seemingly, let alone from Stamford."

"And with a strongbox," Fairfax said, "if that is the gentleman who was inside."

"Aye," Sir Edward said, "a close buttoned-up fellow, with spectacles and an ear trumpet—that's how I know him, though I misdoubt I ever said more than good day to him in m'life. Nor did most folk. He had a reputation for—Well, 'tis no time to speak ill of the man."

"The strongbox . . ." Fairfax mused. "Is it not the case, Mr. Quigley, that most coach proprietors demand an extra premium on luggage, goods, and so on, above a certain value?"

"Oh, surely. If a passenger carries goods with him above the value of five pounds, we make a register of it, and ask for a small consideration. In case of loss or damage, you know. But there's nothing entered here," the innkeeper said, gesturing at the ledger.

"Devilish odd," Sir Edward said. "I'd have thought Twelvetree the last man in the world to be careless of such things."

"He certainly took care to go armed," Fairfax said.

"Mercy on us," Mr. Quigley said, mopping his brow. "Mr. Twelvetree—meeting such an end, on the *Flyer*! I'm dreaming in my bed—I must be . . ."

"No help for it, Quigley," Sir Edward said briskly. "You ain't responsible; that gallows bird of a highwayman is. Come, what are the other names?"

Mr. Quigley consulted the ledger. "Mrs. Parry, inside, to St. Neots. Paid, sixteen shillings, on the fifth of October."

"Now that lady I recall," old Jacob said eagerly. "Came in yesterday to book it herself. A young sort of lady, I think." He put an unsteady hand to his lips. "Leastways, a lady; and she paid from her purse."

"But this makes no sense, " Sir Edward said, frowning. "She was going to St. Neots? But that lies farther than the place the coach was found—past Huntingdon. She . . ." He shrugged in bafflement. "She must have been on the coach when it was attacked."

"Attacked!" murmured old Jacob piteously, and made a stagger to his stool. He was actually taller sitting down than standing up.

"But not a sign of her," Fairfax said. "Unless she never boarded the coach."

"No, she's marked," the innkeeper said, "see here—a tick. The coachman always gives the number of his load before he sets off—it's a thing I insist on at the George, any-how. I've known some dishonest coachmen who'll accept a fare privately, and pocket the money—taking a bit of fish, they call it. No, the *Flyer* set out from here this morning with two inside and one out, that's certain."

"Then where's this woman?" Sir Edward said. "Could it be she escaped harm, and ran away for help when the coach foundered? It seems unlikely. No doubt she'll turn up, if so. Quigley, have you servants you can spare here? It might be as well to send along the road, to Stilton, Alconbury—any-where there might be news of her. Also to discover any more passengers who were to join the coach at those places. 'Tis curious indeed. I don't know any Parrys, do you Quigley?"

The innkeeper shook his head. "You recollect anything more of this lady, Jacob?"

The old man looked lugubrious. "Ah, dear! I wish I could. I don't take a deal of notice of faces as a rule. I'm al-ways so careful with my ciphering, and reckoning the money, y'see, sir—'tis a great trust, and so I keep my head bent over it. A lady—and she paid from a purse—and I'd say pretty. Only at my time of life"—he gave a vague rattle of humor—"there aren't many as *don't* look pretty. Mind you," he muttered, "there's old Nan Digglin who does the linen—she's ugly enough to wean a foal, even to me—"

"Well," Sir Edward said impatiently, "whoever and wher-ever this Mrs. Parry is, at least she escaped the fate of the others, thank God."

"Unless," Fairfax said, "she was on the coach when it was held up, and did not escape. It is an awful thought, but this highwayman may have considered her as part of his spoils."

"What?" Sir Edward stared at him. Then his mouth went tight. "I was going to say he cannot be such a beast—but who knows what he is not capable of? Quigley, send your servants as soon as may be. We must alert the local consta-bles too—everyone. Cock's life, this grows darker."

Another notion occurred to Fairfax just then, though he decided to keep it to himself. It involved the mysterious Mrs. Parry going, not forcibly, but willingly, away with the attacker. An accomplice? Mere irresponsible speculation, of course; and he felt faintly disgusted with himself at the way his mind was eagerly fingering the pieces of this bloody puzzle.

"What of the outside passenger?" he said.

"Mr. Griggs," the innkeeper read out, "for Eaton Socon, paid seven shillings on the fifth of October."

"I remember a man yesterday," old Jacob said. "Not a gentleman, I think, just a quiet, decent sort of man, paid for an outside place . . . I'd remember more if I could," he said in a tone of anxious explanation, "only I can't."

"Wait a moment—Griggs—wasn't that the name of that damned preacher we met?" Sir Edward asked, echoing Fairfax's thought.

"Henry Griggs," he said. "Odd. Not that the surname is so very uncommon."

"Not so common neither," Sir Edward said. "We'd better see what the preacher knows too. Quigley, you must send to Huntingdon also, to the Bridge there. A man named Griggs was about the place, preachifying on all sides. With luck he'll not have gone far, for his horse was near lamed. Well, there's nothing more you can tell us, I daresay, my good man?"

"I would if I could," old Jacob said, seeming to have taken a liking to this formula, "only I can't, sir."

"So, we have Crabbe, the coachman, deceased, poor fellow. We have an outside passenger called Griggs, likewise; Twelvetree, inside, one of our most prominent citizens, likewise, and robbed; and a Mrs. Parry, who was supposed to be inside, but has disappeared into thin air." Sir Edward raised an eyebrow at Fairfax. "A pretty kettle of fish, eh, Fairfax?"

It was, Fairfax thought; and the fish had a mighty odd smell about them too.

While Mr. Quigley sent his servants on their various errands on the fastest mounts the George's huge stabling could offer, Sir Edward sought out the postilion of their post chaise. He dispatched the lad the few miles to Cheyney Hall with a written message, saying that he had been delayed on the road, and telling the steward to send his carriage over to Stamford.

"After that, back to Huntingdon with you, and my compliments to your master," Sir Edward concluded, giving him a heavy tip. The lad looked as if he had aged ten years today. "Now, Fairfax, I think we've earned a mug of ale."

They drank it in a quiet corner of the dim stone-floored taproom. Sir Edward placed a shilling on the tabletop and spun it idly.

"What think you of this business, Fairfax?" His voice was unusually tentative.

"As you say, Sir Edward, there is a most ruthless and stone-hearted killer abroad."

"But you do not think it a simple matter of a highway robber stepping out and taking his chance with the first coach that came along. Come, man," Sir Edward said as Fairfax hesitated, "it's written all over your face. Now, as it happens I'd heard of your exploit with your last pupil, when I sought you out. Young whelp found himself accused of a most appalling crime, ain't that so? And you tracked down the real culprit yourself. Rather remarkable."

"Well, I was terrified of my pupil's father," Fairfax said awkwardly. "Self-preservation can be a great spur."

"Nonsense. You must have a feeling for these things. Your father was a famous judge, wasn't he?"

"More notorious than famous," Fairfax said. "He was disgraced, and took his own life." Blurting it out crudely, he found, was as good a way as any: the pain was got over quickly, though it was no less intense.

"Ah? Well, well. No reflection on you. You know, one of my ancestors in the Tudor days was born on the wrong side of the blanket. Sired a dozen bastards himself, and was the most rascally pirate and adventurer."

Fairfax smiled. Though it was not the same thing, Sir Edward meant well.

"Anyhow, you can't deny you're a man with a nose for

such things. Now, I mean what I say: I shan't rest till I have whoever did this standing before me on the Bench, so that I can send him to the assize, and the appointment with Jack Ketch he deserves. But in the matter of finding him, two heads are better than one—especially if there is more to this man than initially appears."

"And that is what you believe?"

"At first I did not. But now that we know a little of the passengers on that coach . . . This business of the missing woman perplexes me .And as for that poor wretch Twelvetree—that surprises me greatly. At least, to find him traveling so—alone, and armed with pistols, of all things, and apparently carrying something of particular value."

"It is not his habit?"

"I don't know much of his habits, beyond the fact that the man's practically a recluse. Oh, not that he ain't a figure in the town—far from it. Some might say he has altogether too much influence—a finger in every pie, at least as far as his financial interests go."

"Would you say that yourself, Sir Edward?"

The baronet scowled at him. "You needn't cross-examine me, damn it. I don't bank with him, but I've nothing against him. Nothing beyond my usual feeling for these burghers who go shooting up into wealth. They think everything can be bought with money—gentility, respect, position, even men's souls—just a matter of cash over the counter. Of course there's always a sniff of antagonism between the landed interest and the townspeople in a place like this. Take a man like Twelvetree, with bottomless coffers and endless ambition, and he soon starts trying to carve out his own kingdom. Investing in property, even in land—and buying out men with a longer pedigree than he. They say he drives a sharp bargain. I don't say I've heard of anything actually underhanded on his part, but he's never been popular."

"So he was a man with enemies?"

"Show me the man without. But I don't think he will be much mourned."

"Well, it's entirely probable that a highway robber, gathering intelligence on potential travelers in the way they do, should decide on the *Flyer* as his target; a well-known banker on board, and likely to offer rich pickings, even if our man didn't know about the strongbox. Of course, it may be that the strongbox, and whatever was in it, was the attacker's whole and single aim. Mr. Twelvetree's people can perhaps enlighten us there. But why should he kill this man Griggs also? An attempt on Griggs's part to escape is certainly possible . . . yet it seems more unlikely as I think of it. Griggs, perched on the roof, had seen the coachman shot in the head. Wouldn't a rational man seek to put up his hands and surrender rather than risk a scramble to nowhere with an armed assailant behind him?"

"True indeed. Unless the first shot hit Griggs, though aimed at the coachman. Griggs, on the roof, would be directly behind the coachman's seat."

"That's a possibility," Fairfax said thoughtfully. "But then the question of this Mrs. Parry, as you remark, is a curious one. Either she was on the coach when it was attacked, or she was not—it would certainly seem she boarded it here—and both alternatives are mysterious. I suppose there would be nothing to prevent her leaving the coach at an earlier stage?"

"Nothing, except for the fact that she had herself booked and paid for a seat to St. Neots, a good way on. Why get down earlier? Unless an indisposition, perhaps—women don't greatly thrive in the jostle of a public coach. I remember my poor wife was always as sick as a cushion on the road, no matter how gently we went. Well, if that's the shape of it, we should soon know. The lady will surely come forward when she hears she's being sought all over the country. As for this Griggs, if our preacher friend can't enlighten us, someone must know him. Which leaves Twelvetree. I wonder if rumor has reached his house yet. Not a fitting way for a man's death to be announced, I fear, even for a solitary fish like him."

"Is it near at hand? I could carry the news of what has happened, if you like. Sir Edward Nugent's secretary would surely be credited."

"A good notion. Lord knows what tales will be started otherwise. I'd best wait here in case there's news. But it's only a step to Broad Street. I'll point you on the way. And perhaps once there, you might smoke out a few things: what was in the strongbox, and why Twelvetree got on at Wansford instead of here—pertinent things, you know. That is, of course"—Sir Edward stopped spinning the coin and looked dryly at Fairfax—"if you have a fancy to join me in delving into this matter. It was no part of your commission when I hired you, of course, and you may not relish it."

Fairfax smiled. "I think you already know me better."

Following Sir Edward's directions, Fairfax crossed the river bridge into the town, a busy, prosperous place: small wharfs and warehouses visible on the river, much foot and horse traffic, brewers' drays, water carts, private carriages, even one of two sedan chairs. A medley of bow-fronted stone houses, with plenty of crowded shop windows and cellar workrooms; some buildings of venerable age, with tiny casements and bulging walls; and a medieval almshouse, handsome as an Oxford college. Among these, fine tall town houses of a more recent date, evidently residences of gentry. Quite an inviting piece of civilization, this place, with its spires pricking the dark satin blue of the autumn afternoon, yet a place of contrasts too, quite as much as the grand and grim metropolis from which he had come.

In an alleyway off Broad Street, a couple of prentice boys were enjoying the torment of a cat and a dog that they had tied together by their tails. Whooping, grinning, button-eyed, their faces looked both empty and full of purpose. The small incidental cruelty gave Fairfax pause, in spite of, or perhaps because of, the more shocking sights he had seen today. Was this mankind, truly revealed? Sir Edward Nugent, in his cool aristocratic way, would no doubt grunt tolerantly, say that idle and untaught youth were always prone to such things, and box their ears. Someone like the Methodist preacher they had met earlier, though, would draw a more strenuous moral: that nothing we did was unimportant, that the state of our souls appeared in our every action—that here, in fact, was evil. Perhaps that was why such men were unpopular: they made you choose.

Fairfax soon found the place he sought: it bore the name "N. Twelvetree" on a brass plate by the front door. It was a large five-bayed town house fronted by garden walls and a gate with ball-topped piers; there was an older side wing attached, with a great stone gable. An imposing place, though there was something severe and frigid about its aspect too.

Fairfax mounted the steps and rapped on the door, wondering greatly at the position he found himself in—bringing the news of the death of a man he did not know to a house where there were apparently no loved ones to mourn him.

A manservant opened the door to him, and ushered him into a spartan gray counting house, more like a tank than a room. There was a row of pigeonholes, a bureau, and two high desks occupied by two clerks on spindly stools, quill pens wagging. One was a beardless boy; the other, an elderly man all in snuff brown with a scratch wig and an ingratiating tilt to his birdlike head, got down and softly inquired of Fairfax how he might serve him.

"My name is Fairfax. I am secretary to Sir Edward Nugent, of Cheyney Hall. Traveling up to Stamford today, Sir Edward and I—came upon some unfortunate news which must be urgently conveyed to Mr. Nicholas Twelvetree's household. I would say his nearest kin—though I understand there are none."

The clerk inclined his head to an even meeker angle. "I am Mr. Twelvetree's chief clerk, sir. Claymount by name. If I can be of any assistance, sir? Or perhaps, if it is a matter of urgency, I might step up and find out if Mr. Twelvetree will see you himself?"

"Dear me, I'm afraid there is some mistake. The news concerns Mr. Twelvetree himself, you see. The coach in

which he set out this morning met with an accident, a most
tragic accident . . ." Fairfax found himself in some bewilderment as the little man's mild face assumed an almost
disdainful look, but he plunged on. "I have to inform you—
Sir Edward has charged me with informing you—that Mr.
Twelvetree was killed as a result."

The clerk blinked, pursed his lips, and said, "Is that all?"

Was that all? What did the man mean?

"Perhaps, Mr. Claymount, I have not made myself plain."

"Oh, you have, sir, you have. We have not the honor of
counting Sir Edward Nugent among our clients, but I cannot
conceive that he would be party to such a poor jest, and can
only conclude that it is of your own invention. If so, then
you must forgive me—I am quite out of the fashion, sir, no
doubt, but I think it a poor jest, a poor jest indeed."

"Why on earth," Fairfax said almost wildly, "should you
suppose I would say such a thing in jest?"

"Why? I hardly think I owe you an answer, sir, but if you
insist, I will say, because Mr. Twelvetree is this very moment upstairs in his drawing room, quite well but for a little
tisick, and I know this because I spoke to him but fifteen
minutes ago."

Three

Fairfax's utter surprise and bewilderment must have been plain on his face, so much so that the clerk relented somewhat.

"Sir," he said, "really there must be some species of misunderstanding here. I mean no disrespect to you, or indeed Sir Edward Nugent, but I must ask you, is it not possible that you have been gravely misinformed?"

"Something is certainly amiss." Fairfax said, recovering himself. "That fact is, we came upon the wreck of the *Stamford Flyer* ourselves. A passenger had been killed, and the booking office at the George identifies him as Mr. Twelvetree. The body of the dead man is this moment being laid out at the Cross Keys—a black-clad man of about middle height, slender, wearing a full wig and spectacles."

The clerk's eyes grew large.

"Dear, dear. Perhaps," he said, bobbing his little head in agitation, "it would be best if you spoke to Mr. Twelvetree yourself. I'll just step up, sir, if you would be good enough to wait . . ."

After a short interval, which the boy clerk occupied by staring full at Fairfax with no more self-consciousness than a baby, Mr. Claymount came tripping back. Mr. Twelvetree, he announced, would see him in his private apartments upstairs. His tone suggested that this was a favor rarely granted.

A provincial banker was often a merchant or other man of business. Trading in large amounts of goods and sums of cash, and possessing a highly credit-worthy name, he could become almost by default a clearinghouse for the financial transactions of a district. With enough weight and confidence he could become, as was plainly the case with Mr. Twelvetree, a banker proper, looking after the deposits of customers and even issuing banknotes, though these were seldom accepted far afield from the town he lived in. A greater measure of wealth and social eminence might result, and many men, of course, wanted these. Another result of banking was power. Following the clerk upstairs, Fairfax wondered what Mr. Twelvetree's chief motive was.

The room into which Fairfax was shown was plain rather than sumptuous. More striking was the fact that it was approached via an anteroom, with the clerk having to unlock both doors with keys; and the fact, which only dawned on Fairfax after the first few minutes, that it was the cleanest room he had ever been in. He was a fastidious man himself, but he had never known floorboards so scoured and polished, such a glare of whitewash, such a hygienic neatness in everything from the fire irons in the cold marble grate to the platoon of pens, wafers, penknife, and sandbox ranged along the top of the walnut desk that stood in the exact center of the room; and he did not think he could have lived with it.

"This it the—the *gentleman*, sir," the clerk said with a kind of impressive quaver, as if in ushering in Fairfax he was introducing the very devil himself. He left them, with a rattle of locks. Fairfax saw that there were bolts on the inside of the door too.

A thin, high-shouldered man dressed in black was standing by the window, his long hands clasped before him. He was starring at Fairfax just as voraciously as had the boy downstairs, but in this man's eyes there was alarm.

"I have the honor of addressing Mr. Nicholas Twelvetree?"

"You do."

"Sir, forgive me for troubling you with this strange errand. I confess myself somewhat perplexed also. My name is Fairfax, and I came here on behalf of my employer, Sir Edward Nugent, as the bearer of news which—which I see cannot be true."

"My clerk has told me of it." Mr. Twelvetree stepped forward, his eyes still riveted on Fairfax. Just as the room suggested an indifference to luxury, the banker's appearance was not that of a man who wished to dazzle socially. His coat and tight-wound stock were drab, and there was a certain gracelessness about his grasshopper frame and lean, whey-colored, sharp-nosed face. So power's his motive, then, thought Fairfax; then reproved himself for such hasty judging.

What was more notable about Twelvetree's appearance, though, was its resemblance to the dead man in the coach. The same full, old-fashioned frizzed wig; the same small spectacles. And as Fairfax opened his mouth to speak again, Mr. Twelvetree reached in his pocket and drew out an ivory ear trumpet.

"A moment, sir. I have an infirmity in my left ear. I must hear you plain." The cocked ear trumpet, the clipped parsimonious speech with a faint lisp, added to the impression of an elderly man. But a closer view convinced Fairfax that Nicholas Twelvetree was at most forty-five, and not without vigor. "If I understand aright, you claim that my name was entered as a passenger on the *Stamford Flyer.*"

"I have seen it in the booking-office ledger," Fairfax said, not liking the tone of that *claim.* "Sir Edward Nugent and I came upon the *FLyer* at Stangate Hole. It was half in the ditch; the coachman and the passengers had been shot to death, presumably by a highwayman. On reaching the George, we consulted the booking office. Your name was there." He hesitated. "Indeed, the passenger inside the coach appeared . . . he bore a resemblance to yourself. Sir Edward, knowing you but slightly, took him as such, and as a stranger here I could not know otherwise. The man was also in possession of a strongbox, which had been broken open."

He certainly had Mr. Twelvetree's attention. The banker's eyes bulged fishlike behind the spectacles, and his mouth dropped open. Fairfax felt quite at a loss himself. What could it all mean?

"And so," he concluded, "I came here as the bearer of dreadful news, as I thought. Yet . . . I suppose there is no one else bearing your name, sire, who this might be?"

"Hardly." The hand holding the ear trumpet had begun to tremble violently. Mr. Twelvetree stalked over to a side table, poured himself a glassful of something from a decanter—some sort of watery cordial—then sat down by the cold fireplace, leaving Fairfax standing. "I have no family. Besides, my name is known . . . You saw this with your own eyes?"

"Assuredly. You—or your name—had been booked two days since as an inside passenger on this morning's coach to Huntingdon, though to join the coach at Wansford, the next stop, rather than here in Stamford."

Again that thorough-going stare. Well, Fairfax thought, it must be the devil of a shock to find yourself apparently shot dead by a highwayman.

Or by anyone, come to that. And now Fairfax mentally framed the question that, he guessed, was revolving in Mr. Nicholas Twelvetree's mind: Was this a simple matter of a highwayman and his casual victims? Or something altogether more sinister, pointed?

Certainly the banker was not taking this strange news in any philosophical spirit. There were beads of sweat on his narrow brow that were not called forth by any heart in this cheerless room. With a jerk he pulled out a large snowy handkerchief and held it to his nose, adding a camphor smell to that of the scented pastilles burning on the mantelshelf and the bunch of medicinal herbs on the desk.

"I made no such booking," he said. "Nor did any of my servants. I can answer for that."

"The man at the coach office was not sure, but he thought it was a clerk who—"

"Also impossible. I know my staff. What is more, sir, I seldom travel abroad, being vulnerable in health. This whole business is a mistake . . . though what manner of mistake I cannot conceive." The banker gave Fairfax a sharp, suspicious glance. "What did you mean by this man's resemblance to me?"

"The dead man was dressed much like you. He wore spectacles and had an ear trumpet about him."

No wonder that the clerk had viewed him as some sick hoaxer. This was rather horrible. Just as Fairfax found himself pitying Mr. Twelvetree, his eye strayed to a painting above the mantelshelf. It was a portrait in oils of the banker himself, done by a journeyman artist, judging by the rather stiff technique and unsophisticated color. And yet that unknown painter, used no doubt to turning out likenesses of provincial gentry by the dozen, had responded to and caught something highly individual in his sitter. Fairfax sensed the heat of a tremendous will in Nicholas Twelvetree, and the painter had found the spark of it in that awkward, intent face. The portrait was of a man about to make a bargain—forever, instinctively, always about to make a bargain—perhaps even with his namesake, Old Nick himself.

Then Fairfax noticed a much smaller portrait, of a woman, hanging to one side; but Mr. Twelvetree spoke before he could give attention to it.

"Then this booking was made in my name by someone else—for who knows what purpose, what imposture . . ." In a self-communing way Twelvetree wrapped his coat around his thin frame, tapped his lips with intelligent fingers. "Some jest? A very elaborate one. I have no acquaintance of a jesting turn of mind. I am little disposed to society . . . A highwayman, you say, sir? Stangate Hole is a notorious bad spot, and I hear has been much plagued by one of these criminals of late."

"A highwayman, it would appear," Fairfax said. "Unless,

Mr. Twelvetree, you can think of any other explanation for this shocking event."

"I? It has naught to do with me, sir. I was ignorant of this whole matter until"—he actually consulted his watch—"twelve minutes ago. You have no reason to think otherwise, sir."

"Well," Fairfax said placatingly, "doubtless there is some explanation, which will appear in due course. Sir Edward, as a magistrate, is resolved to have the matter fully investigated, and the culprit brought to book."

Again the banker studied him. Then he tucked away the handkerchief and was brisk. "Most naturally. And though, I repeat, I have absolutely no knowledge of this matter, I shall exert all influence in my power to assist. This person must indeed be caught quickly." Pacing, he turned on Fairfax. "But what is being done? The constables alerted? The magistrates? Are we all to be murdered in our beds?"

"I think this particular malefactor confines his attention to travelers," Fairfax said. "But as I said, Sir Edward is determined on his capture. There is already a price on the man's head, and Sir Edward speaks of adding to the sum."

"Really? Then," Mr. Twelvetree said after a thoughtful moment, "I shall too. Dear, dear. To think . . . And others killed too." Very much an afterthought. "Stangate Hole. And Wansford was the place, you say, where this—person presumed to be me boarded the coach? Extraordinary. This person—I shall need to know, sir, who has been making free with my name. Very regrettable no doubt if the person is deceased, but you must consider my position. I need to know what has been going on."

"Dr. Tuplin is examining the remains now. I daresay some identification will be made soon enough. There is sure to be a coroner's inquest tomorrow, if you wish to—"

"I cannot attend." The banker was curt, gnawing his lip. "I do not stir abroad—almost never. I must take care of myself. I cannot expose my health at such a—public place." He went to the window again and ran his long questing fingers along the sill, as if testing it for security.

A frightened man, thought Fairfax. But then, it was alarming news. He tried to put himself in the banker's position. Someone turning up at his door, informing him that a person called Robert Fairfax, answering very much to his description, had been killed in an attack on a stagecoach . . . It would feel strange beyond words: a cheese nightmare, an opium dream.

It would be a matter of utter disbelief, in fact—in a way that it did not seem, quite, for this man.

"Well, Mr. Twelvetree, I'm sorry to intrude so unpleasantly on your time. I'm sure you may easily come by any information that you require, by applying to the George. I may tell Sir Edward you intend to add to the reward?"

"You may. Fifty guineas. Pounds, call it, rather. Fifty pounds," Mr. Twelvetree said, nodding in his self-communing way.

"And there is no information I may offer on your behalf to the magistrates?" Fairfax trod delicately. "You have no notion of who or what might be behind this curious deception—if deception it is?"

Nicholas Twelvetree, over his scented handkerchief, gave Fairfax a last transfixing stare, as if to commit his image to memory.

"None." He let it drop, a clipped halfpence of a word.

Fairfax went to the door, glad enough to get out: the medicinal smells were making him feel a little queasy. As he reached for the handle, however, Mr. Twelvetree spoke again.

"You cannot get out."

Of course, it was locked; he knew it, and the banker knew he knew it. Yet still Fairfax had an odd feeling that Nicholas Twelvetree enjoyed, even relished, saying it.

He waited while Mr. Twelvetree first rang the bell, then unlocked this door and then the door of the anteroom with a great bunch of shining keys. Another manservant had appeared in answer to the bell, hulking and beetle-browed and warty as a toad. Fairfax wondered if there was a half decent-looking person in the whole house.

"Starkey, return here when you have shown Mr. Fairfax out. I would speak with you urgently."

With a rapid jangle of keys, Nicholas Twelvetree locked himself in again.

An odd fish indeed, Fairfax thought as he made his way back to the George. More spider than fish, though—spinning his financial webs from the comfortless nest . . . Then he ruefully acknowledged his own prejudice. He had seen not a single book in that room, and though he had seen so little of the house apart from closed doors, he imagined the same throughout. Now if he was as wealthy as Twelvetree obviously was, he would line his walls with books, and pay homage to them from the comfort of a great wing chair with a full decanter of the choicest Madeira at his elbow . . . But he was not wealthy; he was not Nicholas Twelvetree; and people were various, Fairfax reminded himself. Anyhow, there was no reason to suspect that the banker was telling anything but the truth when he claimed to know nothing of this coach booking made in his name. Indeed, the more he thought about it, the more unlikely it seemed that a wealthy man of retiring habits would travel alone on an unguarded coach, carrying a conspicuous strongbox. With the road to Huntingdon known to be haunted by a notorious highwayman, it would be foolhardy.

In fact, it was almost an invitation.

Fairfax thought about that, and about the pistols in the dead man's hands, as he passed beneath the great gallows-sign of the George. A voice suddenly stirred him from reflection.

"Sir. Sir, I am wanted, I believe."

It was preacher, Henry Griggs, calling out to him. He was mounted now, his horse reshod, though the animal was coming up the south road at a weary plod. Patting its neck, Griggs got down and let it by the bridle.

"I came as fast as I could. A message from your master reached me at Huntingdon."

"My . . . ?" After a bitter moment Fairfax swallowed it. The consciousness of what he was and what he had been, the pricking reminder of his dark fortune, was always liable to come upon him like this. "Ah, yes, Sir Edward."

"It was lucky. I was still at the inn awaiting the shoeing of my horse."

"You know what has happened Mr. Griggs?"

"I have the drift of the tale: naught else is talked of in Huntingdon just now. I passed the wreck of the coach on my way here. There are people gathering on the road like carrion crows, to look. I tremble for them." He shook his head, austere, pale-eyed. "I came, because I understand there is a belief I might know something of one of the victims, though I do not see how this can be."

They went into the inn yard.

"It appears, from the register at the booking office," Fairfax said, "that one of the dead passengers bears the same surname as yourself. I hope . . ." He did not know how to go on. Griggs had stopped dead. The grave pallor of the preacher's face had turned to chalk. Fairfax had never seen a living man so utterly white. "I hope, indeed, that your errand is a futile one."

The preacher put a hand momentarily to his side, with a faint grunt, as if he had been struck. "Pray God it is so," he said with an effort. "But—whatever He wills."

"You have a relation who . . . ?" Again Fairfax couldn't go on. He had not expected this; and Griggs was a hard man to offer sympathy to.

"I have a relation." Griggs closed his lips tightly, glanced around him as if just coming out of a daze, then signaled to an ostler. "I must stable my horse . . . Sir, are the remains laid here? I must see of course. I must see with my own eyes."

"The . . . the dead were taken to the Cross Keys, a little way from here. A doctor was with them." As he spoke Fairfax saw, in the diamond-pained window of the coffee room, the leonine head of Sir Edward, and with him, Dr. Tuplin. "I see the doctor now. If you will follow me . . ."

"Ah, Fairfax." Sir Edward was polishing off a plate of cold meats. "Here's the damnedest thing. Tuplin tells me that poor butchered fellow in the coach *wasn't* Twelvetree at all. I says to him, but we've looked at the register. But no, turns out Tuplin's doctored Twelvetree in his time and knows his looks well."

"The deceased was a younger man," said Dr. Tuplin, who was taking brandy, "and local, I fancy. I think I know him by sight, though not as a patient. But he was certainly dressed much in the manner of Mr. Twelvetree."

"Yes," said Fairfax, "I have just seen that gentleman. I have never brought a man such odd news before."

"Seen him, eh? There's not many as gets an audience. The fellow's as close as an oyster," Sir Edward said. "Well, what had he to say to this diabolical business? Grows rummer all the time."

"He was—concerned, as one might expect. As is Mr. Griggs here." Fairfax presented the preacher, whose face was now stony. "He has come in answer to your request, and is under some apprehension, finding that Griggs is the name of the other victim, that—"

"I must see the body." Griggs addressed the doctor; he had not even glanced at Sir Edward. "Will you show me?"

"Certainly," Dr. Tuplin said, rising. "I should warn you, sir, if you think to make an identification, that the sight may be somewhat distressing."

Fairfax remembered the shattered face of the outside passenger, staring at the sky. Then he remembered the gibbet, and the crow—and quickly banished the thought of what horrors there might have been if the dead had lain there longer.

"I must see the body," Griggs repeated.

"You have kin in these parts, my friend?" Sir Edward said, softening his tone.

"All men are kin," Griggs said, with a bare glance, and turned to the doctor again. "I am ready, sir."

Fairfax and Sir Edward went with them to the Cross Keys, an old low-eaved tavern of stone and thatch with a capacious yard. There, among the barrels, stood the unmistakable form of a bier; there was a hammering in an outhouse. Let us eat and drink; for tomorrow we shall die, thought Fairfax grimly.

The laying-out room was at the rear, down a short flight of brick steps. Fairfax had seen enough, and was glad he did not have to go in. For an instant, it seemed that Henry Griggs would not go in either. He hesitated at the top of the steps, and swayed a little.

"Steady, friend," said Sir Edward, and offered his flask. "Take a nip to strengthen you."

"That is weakness, not strength," Griggs said. His face was still entirely without color. He took a deep breath and followed the doctor in.

"Bah, there's no doing anything with the fellow," Sir Edward said, shrugging and taking a nip himself. "Well, if it is some kin of his lying there, then that's one conundrum solved."

"Yes," said Fairfax uncertainly. "But again, it's curious. He said he could hardly see how it could be anyone he knew, then it was as if some thought came upon him. As if he concluded something . . . Yet Griggs is after all not that uncommon a name. And if he were expecting a relative to be traveling on the *Flyer,* he would surely say so."

"Well, perhaps—though he's too damnably stiff-necked to say anything much. But what's this hare you're starting, Fairfax? Some preacherly plot? Perhaps good Mr. Griggs doing a little highway robbery in between the prayerfests? In which case what has he done with this Mrs. Parry? Nay, man, you're overfinicking."

Fairfax smiled. "I daresay. But as you remarked, Sir Edward, it grows rummer all the time. I was most curiously struck by Mr. Twelvetree. He seemed horribly frightened—

and yet not greatly astonished by his own death, as it were. Tell me, was Mr. Twelvetree ever married?"

Before Sir Edward could reply the door opened.

Henry Griggs walked past them, across the wainscoted passage, into the dingy little taproom. He sat down heavily on a stool and it seemed, from his whole attitude, that he must bury his head in his hands. And yet he arrested the movement, as if with a flexing of will. He placed his hands on his knees—square, roughened, yet not coarse hands— and stared ahead of him. The preternaturally blue eyes were, Fairfax saw, filmed each with a tear precise and translucent as the cover of a watch.

Dr. Tuplin, somber, said, "Mr. Griggs had identified the body of the outside passenger as that of his brother."

"Jonathan," Griggs said, and for the first time Fairfax heard tenderness in that sternly musical voice. "His journey was not long. Well—well. Released, after all, from a world of sin. Praise God. The Lord gave, and the Lord hath taken away; blessed be the name of the Lord."

"A bad business," Sir Edward said, frowning. "A shocking business, my friend. Never fear, we will find that murderous dog, and he will be punished, my word on it. Now pray can you shed any light on this matter? Was your brother robbed too?"

Griggs put the back of his hand to his eyes, delicately, composedly. "The things of this world do not concern him now." The publican-undertaker, a little, greasy, eager man, was hovering near; Griggs waved him away.

"There is nothing in the dead man's pockets," put in Dr. Tuplin. "Nothing at all."

"Well, had your brother baggage with him, d'you know?" Sir Edward asked. "If there is anything identifiable taken, we may trace the culprit through it, when he tries to sell it."

"I can't answer such questions about my brother," Griggs said stonily.

"Perhaps when you have collected yourself a little. It was

a bad shock," said Dr. Tuplin, who seemed one of those men born to moderate and mediate.

"The shock is over," Griggs said, "and as you assure me, sir, that my brother's passing must have been swift, then as a Christian I must rejoice, for now he is happier than we can be." With his habitual mild truculence, he gazed at each in turn, then went on, "I cannot give you the information you seek, because I had no notion that my brother would be on that coach. I can tell you about him, if you wish. His name was Jonathan Griggs, and he was thirty-two years old, seven years my junior. Our parents died young, and we were much together till recent years. We lived and labored together, in sober and godly content; Jonathan did not join the connection, but he was always . . . full of God's grace." Again it seemed he would cover his face; again the gesture was suppressed, though with a visible shudder. "I am the last man to question any dispensation of Providence; but still, what happened seemed—seemed hard. Some two and half years ago, my brother lost his reason. He had always been a man of tender and impressible feeling—a child's sweetness—the gentlest creature ever born. There was an unhappy attachment to a girl. What seemed a melancholy fit became . . . a malady of the mind, with no hope of a cure. I would have kept him by me. I resisted what had to be done. But there was no help for it. When he was at his worst, he was not fit to be free. So he was taken into an asylum for lunatics—Mr. Rowe's asylum, at Ryhall, a few miles north of here."

"I know the place," Dr. Tuplin said, nodding. "I am sorry indeed. But your brother recovered, to be released?"

"He was not released. He never got any better," Griggs said bleakly. "He wasn't violent, and he had times when his mind was clear. But he didn't get better. My brother escaped from Mr. Rowe's house three days ago. Mr. Rowe sent a servant over to my house at Eaton Socon directly, to tell me what had happened. He thought—as I did—that poor Jonathan might try to make his way to me. I believe now"— he licked his dry lips—"that it was so."

"Mr. Griggs, outside passenger to Eaton Socon," Fairfax said, remembering the booking-office register.

"Good God," murmured Sir Edward. "But how the devil came he to escape? Was he not properly confined? And how did he come by the money for the coach fare?"

"I chose Mr. Rowe's house because 'tis known for kind usage of its inmates," Griggs said, his brows lowered at the baronet's language. "I have stinted myself to pay for his keep there, rather than see him chained in some parish madhouse. Such poor souls as live at Mr. Rowe's long, and who are not dangerous, have a measure of freedom. They take a turn in the garden; they are encouraged to occupy themselves. Some may walk down to the village, accompanied, of course. Jonathan was always furnished with some money, and with decent clothes. And as I said, his mind would clear sometimes—it was so the last time I visited him, a fortnight ago. 'Twas like a cloud lifting from the sun. Though the cloud always fell again." Something of this same effect was visible on Henry Griggs's face as he talked of his brother. "It would be a simple enough matter to get away, if the fancy came upon him. So, that is why I am abroad this week. I couldn't journey on the Sabbath, of course, so yesterday I rode up to Ryhall to see Mr. Rowe and discover what I could. It was as I thought: Jonathan had been in good case, it seemed, and had been enjoying the garden by himself. And then, over the wall and away. If it was one of his clear times, he may even have wondered why he was there at all. Mr. Rowe was good enough to point me to a cottage in the village where I could have a bed for the night. I was up betimes this morning, and set out to ride southward, taking in Huntingdon on my way to see my brethren in the connection there, and lead them in prayer. I confess too that I—I held a little hope that I might hear word of Jonathan along the road. Perhaps even find him, if God willed it." His eyes fixed almost dreamily on the sanded floor, Griggs added, "He did not."

"It is a grim end to your hope, Mr. Griggs," Dr .Tuplin said quietly.

Griggs's head went up. "I am content. How can I not be? Jonathan is happy."

Fairfax saw a twitch of irritation in Sir Edward's burly shoulders. "But cold-blooded murder must be punished, my friend. And when one of the victims is, begging your pardon, a harmless lunatic, then it sticks in my craw all the worse. He *was* harmless, Griggs?"

"To everyone but himself," Griggs said. "You may ask Mr. Rowe all about it; he will confirm what I say."

Fairfax intercepted a glance from Sir Edward: *your job.*

"I daresay you saw the other poor creatures in there," Sir Edward went on, nodding his head at the laying-out room. "The coachman, and a gentleman who was riding inside the coach. You don't happen to recognize him?"

Griggs shook his head. "I never saw him before. But I am not much in these parts, except when I would visit Jonathan—once a month, twice if I could shift for it. I have my bread to earn. I am a seedsman in a small way, and have a little market garden; my life is simple." He seemed to throw this statement of fact at the bewigged and beruffled baronet like a challenge.

Sighing, sticking out his jaw, Sir Edward said, "Well, I suppose you know no one of the name of Parry? Mrs. Parry. Apparently she was on the coach with your unfortunate brother—yet the deuce knows where she's gone to."

"No. I know no one of that name."

"Might Jonathan, perhaps, have known this lady, Mr. Griggs?" Fairfax put in.

"He knew no ladies. He lived in his own world." All at once Griggs was on his feet. "I think I have told you all I can. Now there are things for me to do. Jonathan must have a burying. The person of this house makes such arrangements, I think . . . ?"

"Nothing of that sort may be arranged till after the coroner's inquest, my friend," Sir Edward said, "which is to be tomorrow. You had best be on hand to testify, as his kin."

Griggs inclined his head. "And then I may have him buried? Because I must soon be on my way. I have promised the brethren at Huntingdon a preaching. I have the Lord's work as well as my own."

"Well, as long as you are here tomorrow," Sir Edward said. "The George, I would suggest, offers comfortable accommodation and a good table."

"For a man of my means and wants," Griggs said austerely, "this place will do, if the man can give me a bed overnight." The publican had popped up again, nodding eagerly.

"Well," Sir Edward said, stumping to the door with barely concealed annoyance, "I thank you for your help, Griggs, and I'm sorry for your brother . . . Insufferable fellow!" he burst out as soon as they were outside. "Like he's swallowed a poker! If these are the godly, give me the devil's party any day of the week."

"He was much affected, I think, by the sight of his poor brother," Dr. Tuplin said temperately.

"The brother I pity. But there's no pitying such a man as that—he'll throw it back in your face. And as for affected— why, I think it's pretty cold, the way he wants to get the poor fellow buried so he can be off to his preaching."

"I think Mr. Griggs's faith is sincere," Fairfax said, "and so he sincerely believes that his brother has gone to a better place—is to be envied, even; and thus his mortal clay is of very little account. All the things of this world are corrupt, and not to be valued a jot. 'Tis a severe sort of belief, difficult for rational men to penetrate." Also, he thought, a repulsive one; but he felt his own touch of envy for it. Such utter certainty must be a great resource. It helped this man view the murdered corpse of his brother without once crying to the skies or swearing vengeance.

Sir Edward grunted, unconvinced. "So, on the coach we have a disappearing woman, a man who seems to be

Nicholas Twelvetree but isn't, and a lunatic from a local madhouse. What do you know of that place, Tuplin?"

"Nothing bad—which, as asylums go, is as good a recommendation as any. I hear the regimen is enlightened, though I have never visited it, and I know of no medical man who has. The asylum-keeper, Mr. Samson Rowe, was, I believe, a physician in the North Country. He took a special interest in diseases of the mind, and opened the asylum with a legacy."

"I have seen Bedlam, of course," Sir Edward said. "A barbarous place. My girls were all a-dangle to go and see it last time we were in London, but I had to be pretty firm. None but a brute could find entertainment in goggling at those poor tormented creatures. I would have the practice forbidden."

"It sounds as if Mr. Rowe's establishment is much more humane," Fairfax said. "One wonders why, indeed, Mr. Griggs's brother should suddenly choose this time, after two and a half years, to make an escape."

"Oh, there's no knowing how the mind of such a poor afflicted soul works," Sir Edward said. "Still, it will be worth our while to talk to this Mr. Rowe."

"You don't trust Griggs's account?"

"My dear fellow, I've served as Justice of the Peace for nigh on fifteen years. I never trust anybody's account of anything."

Evening was descending as they came once more to the inn yard of the George. Lights glowed in the many latticed windows and there was a genial smell of roasting beef. Dr. Tuplin said he would have to leave them now, and while he spoke with Sir Edward on arrangements for the inquest tomorrow, Fairfax found himself gazing at the York coffeeroom window with a wistful sense of being chilled, tired, and hungry.

As he looked, a woman stepped into view, right in the center of the window. She stood there quite still, looking out—at him?—perfectly framed, like a three-quarter-length portrait. She was young, dark-haired and dark-eyed, oval-faced, not very tall though with a well-rounded figure, and she was dressed simply and fetchingly—straw hat, flowered gown with laced stomacher and a crossed white handker-chief over her shoulders. A genre painting, then, stressing nature and light and simplicity, rather than the grand flour-ish of a society portrait.

This fanciful notion so absorbed him that it was startling to see her suddenly move, her hand going up to her face. There was distress in the gesture, perhaps also a sort of com-fort—as if she found reassurance in cupping the lovely shape of her cheek in the palm of her hand. Then, more star-tling, another figure appeared in the frame. A dark stocky young man approached from behind her and tentatively reached out to touch her arm.

She gave such a convulsive jump, turning, that Fairfax jumped in sympathy.

"Handsome creature," Sir Edward said at his elbow. "Now, let's find Quigley. Ah! Here he comes. Well, Quigley, my carriage has arrived, I hope? I think we've done all we can for now, and I'd like to see my home."

"It's here, sir." Mr. Quigley, who was very agitated—al-most dancing on his toes, with the oddly poised delicacy of fat men. "And so is a young woman, come asking after her husband. Lord bless me, in quite a taking she is. I told her you were in charge of the matter and that you'd be here soon. The fact is"—he lowered his voice—"she says her husband took the coach to Huntingdon this morning—the *Flyer*—and hasn't returned."

Four

Quite a taking, Mr. Quigley had said, but when they entered the coffee room, what struck Fairfax about the young woman was her composure. She turned from the window to face them, her hands folded in front of her, and fixed Sir Edward, Mr. Quigley, and Fairfax in turn with a luminous, unblinking gaze. And then Fairfax saw that the composure was more like a gathering in of vast energy. Her breathing was as rapid as a kitten's; her nails shone whiter against the white-pressed skin of her elegant hands.

"My dear, won't you sit down? I am Sir Edward Nugent; my secretary, Fairfax." All courtly gentleness, the baronet steered the young woman into a seat by the fireplace. "As Justice of the Peace, I am looking into this unfortunate affair of the *Stamford Flyer*. You have heard, perhaps, that the coach suffered an accident."

"Molly came to me with some news, or gossip," the young woman said. "My servant girl, that is. It was all round the town. About the *Flyer* being held up by highwaymen . . ." Her voice, light and musical, lost its firmness very suddenly, her hands writhed, yet her gaze did not falter. "And everyone killed."

"We came to find out the truth of it. These things get twisted, don't they? It was the stocky young man whom Fairfax had seen with her in the window; he was hovering at a kind of tenderly respectful distance. "Tom should have been home by now—but there may be any number of reasons why he mightn't, you know . . ."

Sir Edward said, "And you are, sir?"

"This is Mr. Joseph Fox," the young woman said, her voice steady again. "He is a friend and partner to my husband, Tom. I am Barbara Honeyman. My husband is a timber merchant at Water Street. It was with regard to his business that he set out early this morning to go to Huntingdon. He said—last night, that is—he said that he would take the coach."

"The *Flyer*?" asked Sir Edward.

"I believe so—though I cannot recall him saying the name."

"I thought it must be the *Flyer*," Joseph Fox said. "It's the only one I know of. There's the *Daylight* from Grantham, Tuesdays and Thursdays, but that doesn't come to Stamford until about half past ten, and Tom went early. That I can engage for, because I saw him go. 'Twas before six—not even full light. I'd come to the yard early because we were expecting a load of timber by lighters from Spalding. They sail by night when there's a moon. Tom was up and about, said he was coaching it to Huntingdon today. I had my morning draft with him in the kitchen, and off he went. It was mighty early. It's only a step from Water Street to here, and I thought he would have time and to spare before the coach; but he said something about getting breakfast at the George first."

"Did he take anything with him?" Fairfax said.

"He had a small bundle, wrapped in sacking," said the young man. "I don't know what 'twas."

Mrs. Honeyman, at Sir Edward's inquiring glance, said, "I know nothing about that. I wasn't astir when my husband left. He had merely told me last night that he was coaching to Huntingdon on the morrow, and to expect him back by the early evening. I might have felt no anxiety yet, if it were not for these reports—these tales . . ."

"I was at the yard all day, dealing with the timber,"

Joseph Fox put in. "I was just getting ready to go home when Mrs. Honeyman comes out to me with this dreadful tale she'd heard from Molly. The wench is always full of gossip, mind; so I said we'd go round to the coach office and find out the truth of it."

"Mr. Quigley," Sir Edward said, "will you bring a glass of brandy? My dear Mrs. Honeyman, we must look at the facts carefully. I have to tell you that the reports are true: the *Flyer* was attacked, and both coachman and passengers, I regret to say—"

"He's shot—he's shot!" The cry she let out was loud, agonized—yet musical still: the notes, Fairfax's ear discerned, a perfect fifth and seventh.

"Hush, now, ma'am—don't take on," Fox said, looking pained. "We know nothing yet."

"Madam, the identity of one of the passengers is still unknown," Sir Edward said. "He booked his seat on the coach in the name of Mr. Twelvetree, the banker, whom you may know; but the man we found is not Mr. Twelvetree, though there was some superficial resemblance." He glanced at Fairfax a moment; both were thinking the same thought. "Perhaps, Mrs. Honeyman, you could describe your husband?"

"He is—he is a man of six-and-thirty." Barbara Honeyman, whom Fairfax guessed was no more than twenty-three, composed herself again, biting her lips. The biting could add nothing to their redness. "Quite tall, slenderly made, fair—he generally wears his own hair, curled; it sat quite gentlemanly upon him . . . oh I beg you, tell me if it is he. It is the most appalling torture—"

"Does he wear spectacles, ma'am?" Fairfax said.

A startled silence, almost as if he had asked something indecent. Barbara Honeyman stared at him, then at her knotted hands.

She said, "He does not. But last week—last week, Tom brought home a pair of spectacles that he had got at second-hand from the market. He said he fancied his eyes were growing weak and wanted to try if they would help. I did not much like them on him and he put them away . . ." Tears began to bead on her eyelashes. "What is going on? Please tell me . . ."

With another glance at Fairfax, Sir Edward said, "I was going to ask you, Mrs. Honeyman, whether you could think of any reason why your husband should pass himself off as Mr. Twelvetree. But I think what we had best do, if you feel strong enough, is walk over to the Cross Keys. Nothing is certain, I repeat, but equally, I think, nothing can be known until you have viewed the person lying there. It will not be pleasant; it may be the hardest thing you will ever have to do."

Sir Edward's making a dramatic challenge of the request, Fairfax noticed, seemed to have its effect. Mrs. Honeyman looked up, nodded, and rose. Her face was dewy with tears that she did not wipe.

"What about me? Perhaps I could do it. I'm Tom's best friend, and his partner," Fox said, keeping watchfully at Mrs. Honeyman's side.

"You also, perhaps, sir," Sir Edward said, "but Mrs. Honeyman, as next of kin, must make the identification. Or otherwise, my dear," he added gently.

But Barbara Honeyman seemed to need no comforting flannel now: ready, resolved, wanting it over and done. Her step was steady as they made their way back to the Cross Keys, though Joseph Fax still hovered near, as if fearing some collapse. He was a man in his late twenties, dressed in a blue brass-buttoned coat of faintly naval cut, dark and, for all his sturdiness, lithe with an animal vitality; his own black curly hair tied in a queue, large strong restless hands. There was an open obligingness about him, a directness of accent and look. Fairfax had a feeling that he had been at sea.

It was Fox who kept talking nervously as they walked, trying almost desperately to make the best of things. "I keep thinking perhaps he didn't go by the *Flyer* after all. He might have gone by the carrier's wagon—half a dozen of

them a day plying that road. What business he had in Huntingdon I don't know. I leave that side of things to him. Some
builder perhaps. Tom started up the house, you see, and does
the managing and accounting. I put in my little nest egg, a
third share really, and I do the day-to-day business in the
yard. Seasoning and dressing and cutting. Good with my
hands, you see, not so much with my brain. That's Tom. So
I keep thinking the carrier but I don't know . . . He was
dressed rather—well, I can't imagine him sitting in a wagon
among a lot of straw and farmer's chickens. He had on a suit
of a kind of rusty black—very sober-looking, I'd never seen
it before. I joked with him before he went, said he looked as
respectable as a parson, but he just smiled."

"His father's."

Barbara Honeyman, walking just ahead of them, stopped
dead as she spoke these words. Now Fairfax saw how slight
she was, how young. They were just about to cross the street
to the Cross Keys, and a dray was turning in, lumbering, tilt-
ing. It was entirely loaded with the carcasses of ducks and
other wildfowl, plentiful in the nearby fen, and for a moment that whole deathly load—limp necks, daintily stiffened
feet—overshadowed and seemed on the point of toppling
onto her.

"It was an old suit of his late father's. He took it from a
trunk the other day, where it had been laid up in mothballs.
He said it was a pity it should go to waste."

Fairfax met her eyes. In the lamplit evening they were
unfathomable, as befitted the situation.

For this part he had very little doubt now that the unknown man lying in the stone-flagged room at the Cross
Keys was Barbara Honeyman's husband. What curious deception the man had been involved in. Why had he made a
booking in the name of Mr. Twelvetree? Why had he taken
pains to imitate that gentleman's appearance? Why had he
gone to join the coach at the next stage at Wansford? What
had his errand been with a now-empty strongbox? A way to

the answers must be through Barbara Honeyman and Joseph Fox. But first there must be confirmation.

It came, soon enough. Sir Edward gently ushered the lady into the back room of the Cross Keys. There was a single, hollow sob, almost owlish in its tone. Joseph Fox, waiting in the taproom with Fairfax and the ever-eager publican, went white.

Barbara Honeyman came out, supported by Sir Edward. "Brave in you, my dear," he said, helping her to a seat, "damned brave I call it. There, over now . . . Mr. Fox, if you are ready . . ."

Joseph Fox looked far from ready. But he went in, and emerged very soon, trembling.

"Bring me a glass of something strong, will you?" he said to the publican. "Blast my eyes before I see such a sight again. Poor old Tom. God rest him."

"Ma'am, it is your husband, Mr. Thomas Honeyman?" Sir Edward pressed gently.

Weeping silently, the young widow nodded.

"It's Tom," Fox said, swiftly draining the brandy that was brought him, "though I never saw him in such a rum old wig before. My God, I can't believe it. My God." He waggled his glass for more, sweating.

"We shall have the devil who is responsible, ma'am, never fear," Sir Edward said, seating himself near Mrs. Honeyman. "But I think we shall need help. And anything you can tell us that may furnish that help . . . All we know, ma'am, is that the coach was attacked at Stangate Hole sometime before noon. The coachman, name of Crabbe, was killed too, and also a man named Jonathan Griggs; and it seems there was a third passenger called Mrs. Parry—of her fate we know nothing. Are any of those names familiar to you?"

"I don't think so . . . but I can't think . . ." In her distress Fairfax noted that she had reverted to that earlier gesture of self-comfort—holding the shape of her cheek in her hand.

"I never heard of them," Fox said. Brandy had turned his

pallor to a flush. "Why would a highwayman slaughter so? What need was there?"

The pertinent question. Fairfax said, "When we discovered Mr. Honeyman, he had about him a brace of pistols. They had not been fired. Also he had with him a small strongbox, about the size of a jewel box, emptied, presumably by his attacker. You knew your husband possessed such things, ma'am?"

"Yes. Or—no . . . I don't know of any strongbox . . . He bought a brace of pistols, I know, some months ago. I did not like to see them about. But he said it was as well for a man of property to have such things. I don't know why he had them, or why he was dressed so . . . I only know I have lost the best of husbands, and I cannot—I cannot support it . . . I don't know what I shall do . . ." Weeping bitterly, she covered her face.

Fairfax mouthed to Joseph Fox the word *Children*? Fox, after a moment of puzzlement, shook his head.

"I'm greatly sorry, my dear. There is no mitigating such a loss," Sir Edward said feelingly, patting her hand. "I have known it myself. All I can offer is the assurance of Dr. Tuplin, who examined the victims, that the end was entirely swift. Little enough, I know." He nodded at Fairfax, adding, "I think we should trouble you no more with questions. And I think you should go home and take care of yourself. Is there someone who can be with you?"

"Me," said Joseph Fox promptly. "I'll take Mrs. Honeyman home, and stay by her. I'm much about the place anyhow. I thought of poor Tom like a brother if anything."

"You are very good, sir; but I was thinking perhaps a lady to bear you company, Mrs. Honeyman."

"I want no one," she said. "I can be alone. I *am* alone, now"—drawing herself up—"from this moment. It must be faced. Alone—that is me."

It was affecting. Was it also, Fairfax wondered, too readily, consciously tragic? He recalled those melodic cries, *He's shot—he's shot!* And now it occurred to him that no one had said anything about shooting at that point. But of course, news of the *Flyer*'s fate had already got round the town, garbled or not: that was how it had reached her. And at moments of high emotion, one tended to fall into dramatic postures. That was where drama came from, after all.

"There's old Mrs. Raimey next door," Fox said. "She can come in and sit with you, you know."

Mrs. Honeyman seemed not to hear him. She turned the white oval of her face, not to the benignly bending Sir Edward, but to Fairfax. She was utterly charming, he thought randomly. Charming not in the sense of the polite drawing room, where the word was applied to an insincere compliment or a frock with bows, but in its true meaning. In his younger years as a Grub Street hack Fairfax had labored as one of Johnson's assistants, compiling the great *Dictionary*, and words were the furniture of his mind. To charm was to enchant as by a song—which, of course, was where the word *enchant* came from likewise. Chant, canto, cantata. He was willing to bet, suddenly, that Barbara Honeyman was skilled in music. "What about . . . my husband?" she said. "Must I leave him in this place?"

"I think it might be as well," Fairfax said. "The landlord here undertakes such work. And the—other matters must wait until after tomorrow, when the coroner and jury will sit in inquest on the death of your husband and his fellow travelers."

"What does it mean?" Still she turned her intensity on him. "Tom is dead, and murdered, and bloody." Said with a sort of defiance, as if, Fairfax thought, everyone else had pusillanimously shirked these words. "Do they have to take his poor wounds and parade them publicly? And—a jury: 'tis as if he murdered himself—"

"It's to decide the cause of death, and when they've done that, they can look for the villain in earnest," said Fox—rather shortly and irritably, it seemed to Fairfax. "You must see that, Mrs. Honeyman. But I know, it's hard . . ." He shuffled his feet, awkward as a schoolboy.

"Yes, Joseph. It is hard."

"You've not doubt heard, ma'am, of this rogue who's been plaguing the north road in our parts," Sir Edward said. "We have good reason to believe now that he has added murder to his crimes. But he'll suffer for what he's done, ma'am, never fear."

"Hang him," the widow said, in an undertone of chilling conviction. "Hang him up and let people see . . . But what is being done? Isn't this murderer being sought, hunted down? He took my husband—does no one care?"

"Come, Mrs. Honeyman, I'll take you home," Fox said. "You'll do yourself no good here."

Tragically, Barbara Honeyman stood facing the closed door of the beery morgue. A glow of sickly candlelight leaked through the crack beneath, as if it were some last spectral emanation from the dead within. "I have lost the best of husbands," she pronounced tonelessly. "I am alone . . . I must go away. Yes, that is what I shall do. I can't stay in Stamford, with all the memories about me . . ."

"Time is enough to think of that." Again Fox was faintly impatient. "Come."

"Did no one survive?" She addressed Fairfax. "Did no one see this monster?"

"Our task would be easier if so. But no matter," Fairfax said. "Every beast leaves a trail. He will be caught, and justice will be done."

She gave him a challenging look. "And will justice bring back Tom?"

"No."

"Then it's no justice."

A woman always ready to fight her corner, he thought: emotional truth versus male facts.

"Come, Mrs. Honeyman," Fox pressed her, "let's get home with you. It's a raw damp sort of evening. You'll catch cold."

"Why, what could that possibly matter?" she said. A reasonable enough question, Fairfax thought; though again it had the effect of making others, in this case her anxious attendant Joseph Fox, seem clumsy, obtuse, heavy-footed. Watching them go at last, Fairfax thought of another question, and was sure that one of them or both, must know the answer to it: why on earth was Tom Honeyman passing himself off as Mr. Nicholas Twelvetree?

They had done, as Sir Edward said, all they could for now; he was eager to be at Cheyney. At the George his carriage was ready, their luggage in the rumble, so after a few last words with Mr. Quigley they were off on the final leg of their interrupted journey. The carriage took them at a clip out of Stamford, through a pleasant well-settled country of limestone villages, sheep meadows, fields neat as strips of corduroy. The counties of Lincolnshire, Northamptonshire, and Huntingdonshire met here, as did the clay midlands and the eastern fens; the place was like a distilled essence of Shire England. Cheyney Hall stood on the edge of a robust little village called Barnack. Limestone deposits here had led to its being quarried, six hundred years ago, for the building of the cathedral at Peterborough. This explained a curious stretch of landscape that Sir Edward pointed out to Fairfax between the lights of the cottages, a miniature range of heathery hills and hollows, as if a piece of moorland fell had crept down from the north.

The same Barnack stone, Sir Edward told Fairfax proudly, had gone into the building of Cheyney Hall a hundred years ago, with slate for the roof from nearby Colleyweston.

The house presented its face at the end of a long straight avenue of lime trees, like an architectural reflection of its owner, Fairfax thought at first sight: handsome, square, civilized, approachable yet absolutely assured. Rambling wings and Gothic turrets would never have done for Sir Edward. As the carriage drew up on well-raked gravel, Fairfax saw that the house was commodious but not overlarge: two stories, a flat central pediment, three rows of scroll-finished

windows on either side of it, rusticated base and a short
flight of steps to the front door, steep hipped roof with dorm-
ers. Outbuildings in pavilion style, low and retiring. A very
English compromise between classical and domestic.

"Papa! You are here at last, and what a perfect pig you
were not to come before!"

"You're so late, Papa. We were fancying all sorts—at
least Amelia was, being a goose, and she would not heed me
when I said—"

"Goose to you. Letitia was worried too, Papa; she lies—
and did you bring me the shawl that you promised? Only—"

"There is filial duty for you, Papa. The little miss would
rather have a shawl than you—"

"Oh, boh to you, that is the most monstrous—you know
I have been missing him prodigiously, and I only mentioned
the shawl but once, and . . ."

Like an explosion, Sir Edward's daughters had burst
from the house. Laughing, hugely happy, Sir Edward
hugged and kissed them.

"Well, my dears, I am safe, and so is the shawl, and so are
one or two other things that you shall see by and by. And so
is Mr. Robert Fairfax, who is come to work on your grandfather's library. Fairfax, my daughters: Letitia and Amelia."

Shyness utterly extinguished the two girls for a few moments, as they murmured red-faced greetings. Then they
were off again, bearing their father up the steps. At the top,
in a proscenium of candlelight, servants waited; at their
head, a plain woman whom Sir Edward introduced as Mrs.
Hargrave. She was, Fairfax gathered, governess-companion
and general female presence to the girls in the motherless
household. She had the faintly acid skeptical look of one
who spends much time in the company of those who know
everything, in other words: the young. I shall have that look
myself sooner or later, Fairfax thought. And had the little
minxes been good, Sir Edward inquired, his arms affection-
ately round their shoulders? Only one answer, of course.

But then, the girls or young ladies did seem agreeable,

delightful, not much spoiled. Listening to the teasing and counterteasing that went on between them and Sir Edward—"The blue silk, Papa—we ordered it before you went away." "Whatever for, my dear?" "Why, for the Assembly, Papa—you ordered the gown, so we must be allowed to go." "No, no, I know nothing of this, my dears—" Fairfax was conscious of not fitting in. This was family life, foreign country to him now. He felt regret, also comprehension; this was how people harmlessly and productively used up the restless energy that in a solitary being like him was a continual inward ferment. He was glad to be away for a space, shown by a manservant to his room where he could unpack and wash and dress before joining the family for supper. Well, he had certainly been worse accommodated than this in his time: an ample country-house bedchamber, snugly wainscoted and smelling of beeswax, with a wood fire burning. He parted the brocade curtains to look out over the stable yard. Grooms were unharnessing the carriage horses by lantern light; a maid called out a ribald pleasantry from the back door. Beyond, the soft symmetrical shapes of a formal walled garden; then black folds of country, a cold sea around the warm domestic island. Impossible not to think of the bleak high road where three people had met death, sudden and stark. And impossible not to think of that someone—out there somewhere, walking or resting or drinking, certainly living—who had killed today. Fairfax conjured a notional diary entry: *Tuesday, the sixth of October 1761. Today I, whoever I might be, shot to death three people.* It must be graven thus on the mind, if not on a physical page. How did it feel?

Dark thoughts. Going down to supper he dismissed them, or had them dismissed for him; Cheyney Hall, well lit, comfortably gracious, was an Augustan riposte to morbid imaginings. Reason ruled. There was a touch of grandeur about the hall, with busts in niches either side of the great carved staircase, but in the dining room the chill of aristocratic marble extended only to a monumental chimneypiece. The ceil-

ing was molded with restrained festoons, the walls were
hung with crimson damasks and tapestries, the high-backed
chairs were upholstered, and supper was served on a walnut
dining table large enough for ease but not so vast as to make
conversation a matter of hallooing across the empty spaces.
Though Fairfax had lost count of the number of times Sir
Edward had eaten today, he was not surprised to find the
supper substantial and the baronet's appetite undiminished.

Inevitably, the journey's adventure was spoken of. Sir
Edward tried to play it down, said it was no fit subject for
the table. His daughters were having none of that: London,
clothes, the Assembly, the wrongs of Mrs. Hargrave, were
forgotten; this was excitement. We are all ghouls, thought
Fairfax, but the young are not hypocritical about it.

"And you absolutely saw the coach in the ditch, and the
people lying murdered! How vastly awful and thrilling! I
declare I shouldn't be able to sleep for a week for nightmares!" That was Amelia, the younger, who even as she
spoke was eating as heartily as her father.

"That's no wonder. You had nightmares after that foolish
play we were at, with a ghost who was nothing but a man all
chalked, and a handkerchief round his head." Letitia was,
Fairfax remembered, seventeen. The two years' seniority ex-
pressed itself in a selective decorum: she ate little and fas-
tidiously; she kept her back straight; and where her sister
had quite lost her shyness of the stranger, she could not address Fairfax without a pink tinge and a curious arching of
the neck. Her talk, though, was uninhibited. "Papa, do you
suppose the highwayman was watching you from the woods
even then? With his pockets full of his spoils, and his pistols
smoking?"

"My Lord, a highwayman—how monstrous romantic!"
cried Amelia. "With a mask, and pistols and everything, just
like Macheath or Dick Turpin!"

"Macheath was a pretend fellow in a play, my dear," Sir
Edward said. "And Dick Turpin, no matter what the broad-
sheets say, was a cowardly brute."

"Or Claude Duval," Amelia went on, unperturbed, "who asked the lady to dance a galliard with him, and spared her jewels!"

"A Frenchman," Fairfax could not resist saying, "and so, of course, a more mannerly species of robber."

"You would not find it romantic if you had seen what we have seen, my dears," Sir Edward said. "Nor, indeed, did Mr. Devereaux when he was robbed in broad daylight. The friend I told you of, Fairfax; I must have a talk with him and see if he remembers anything useful."

"Then you are going to catch this man, Papa?" Amelia asked.

"A dreadful crime has been committed. As a magistrate, I shall see to it that everything is done to bring the malefactor to justice. Mr. Fairfax shall be my right arm in this, before I turn him loose in Grandfather's library."

"What about the Assembly ball on Saturday, Papa?" Letitia said. "Just think—there will be any number of people coming in to Stamford by carriage. Rich pickings for your villain. Will people hazard it, do you suppose?"

"Well, now, would you, my dears?"

The girls chorused their determination: fir and flood would not stop them, let alone a highwayman . . .

It was fascinating to observe them. In many ways they were very different. Letitia, at a ball, would be no less than a beautiful young woman. Amelia, scarcely less tall, had a child's unmoderated voice and the square-bodiced dress hung flatly on her, as on the jointed dolls that were used by dressmakers. And yet one could see that the elder had looked like the younger only very recently, and that Amelia would very soon resemble Letitia. The effect was as if they were growing and changing visibly, right before one's eyes. It must make a man philosophical, Fairfax thought, to live with it: the hourglass ever running.

Sir Edward did not insist that the men stay at the table with the port when dinner was over, a custom Fairfax always disliked. Instead he proposed that they look over old Sir

Jemmy's library. "Let us see if Mr. Fairfax is daunted, eh, my dears?" He chuckled, an arm about each of his daughters.

The library was actually two rooms, one formerly a music room, with double doors connecting them. A gentleman's library was often a quiet room with some books locked in glass cases, where the gentleman came to get away from his family, perhaps tope or snore. The late baronet of Cheyney Hall had turned his into a Byzantine extravagance of learning, a Babel of books. The deep coving had been removed so that the bookshelves could mount to the very cornice. Like the miser's hoard, it was grand, secretive, illogical. Many volumes were shelved spine inward, the edges of their pages worn shiny and smooth as from fond fingers that had known them by touch. Tables were stacked with slablike folios. Fairfax's hesitant fingers touched incunabula or early books, beautiful monsters from Caxton's day. Codices, horn-bound, the ink seeming as fresh as when it poured from the monastic pen. A treatise on medicines in medieval Latin, together with what was surely the Arabic manuscript from which it had been translated.

"But this is remarkable," Fairfax devoutly murmured. "This, surely, is a first printing of *Le Morte D'Arthur*. And this—this must be a Tyndale New Testament; I thought they were all burned . . ."

Through the double doors, more books, but also many paintings and prints—some, Fairfax judged, mere rubbish, some precious; and seafaring maps, beautiful specimens of Portuguese and Turkish cartography, though surely fanciful in some of their details—landmasses to the south of the Indies, for example. Cabinets of coins, medals, relics. It was overwhelming, almost intimidating; he was glad to find some homely touches here—old maps of the Cheyney estate covered with earthy English place names, and drawings in chalks and pencil by the young Misses Nugent, fondly preserved by Grandpapa. The most recent were very accomplished—the girls had talent and had been well taught—but the older ones started off a lot of mutual teasing, and remarks about squint eyes and six-fingered hands.

They were a close family. Fairfax could not help but feel a touch of melancholy exclusion, perhaps more so when Letitia said to him before retiring, with mingled awkwardness and grace, "I hope you'll enjoy your stay with us, Mr. Fairfax." Always a stay, and then a going!—on to some other illusion of home.

Even the prospect of being let loose in that fantastical library, enticing as it was, could not quite hold off gloom as Fairfax blew out his candle and turned in. "Cerebration, young Robbie," his old mentor, Sam Johnson, used to advise him when in these dark moods. "Exercise the sickly mind as you would a limb." So he set himself to thinking, not of the highwayman whom Sir Edward had resolved they would catch, but of highwaymen in general. What did he know of them? He had never had the misfortune to be held up by one himself, though in London he had had his pocket picked several times, and once had been knocked over the head by footpads in a dark byway. The work of a moment; he had found himself on the ground, without hat or purse, while heavy feet trotted swiftly into the darkness. Not even a glimpse of his assailants.

The robbers who plied the high roads were of a different stamp. They were of necessity mounted and armed. Not for them the casual pickings of a teeming city. Their trade entailed a degree of forethought and also of risk; though commonly masked, they had in a way to go before their public like actors. Main roads, well traveled but not overbusy, were their favorite haunt, and in recent years the number of depredations on the main roads out of London—Hounslow Heath, Gadshill, and Shooter's Hill were particularly notorious— had become something of a scandal. Such places offered, of course, the other necessity for the highway robber, a hideout. Sometimes one heard of cases where the criminal had lived a normal life among unsuspecting neighbors—Fairfax remembered one who had been a respectable farmer—but